My Determined Suitor

Middlemarch Shifters 7

Shelley Munro

My Determined Suitor

Copyright © 2022 by Shelley Munro

Print ISBN: 978-1-99-106308-3
Digital ISBN: 978-0-473-35749-8

Editor: Mary Moran

Cover: Kim Killion, Killion Group Inc.

Munro Press, New Zealand.

First Munro Press electronic publication August 2016

First Munro Press print publication December 2022

For Paul.

Introduction

Every woman has needs. Lana Sinclair, feline shapeshifter and widow, is more than ready for a fun night with a likeminded male. Hot lovin' is compulsory because she's determined to scratch the itch that's driving her crazy. This time, career-girl Lana is picking a malleable male who won't try to corral her into the housewife role.

Fellow shifter Duncan Ross is the perfect candidate. The cowboy follows the rodeo circuit and is only in Middlemarch for the bull riding. One night of mutual seduction, slick, naked bodies and pleasure then he'll be on his way.

Duncan is astonished when Lana propositions him, but no one could ever call him stupid. He's always desired Lana and now that she's ready for sex, he's all action. It's time to lasso the woman of his dreams with some sweet lovin' and charm, a sexy massage and ropes spliced together with addictive pleasure. He'll seduce her to his way of thinking—a permanent arrangement. This is one go-round Duncan is determined to win.

Chapter 1

An Old Friend

A stiff breeze blew over the hill, bringing a rash of chill bumps to Lana Sinclair's naked body. She shuddered despite the burning heat of the sun, dark hair flying loose and wild like a halo around her head. The stark wildness of her surroundings, the gray schist and land burned dry by the hot summer sun, sent an answering emotion skimming across her nerve endings and writhing deep within her soul. It had been so long. So very long. Loneliness crept to the fore.

She missed Jamie, missed spending time with a male, talking and touching. Making love. Her eyes misted while she thought of her mate, killed in a skiing accident at Coronet Peak almost two years ago. Lord, she'd loved that alpha male even though he'd infuriated her with his attitude, especially near the end when they'd been barely speaking. Sometimes she wondered if they would have stayed together, despite both bearing mating marks. Their words had ventured into vicious during the last fight before Jamie had stormed off to go skiing. *Moot point*.

It was time to move on with her life, or at least try living instead of existing. Time to misbehave. Her mating mark had faded, and she was free to choose another.

Richard Saunders, the lawyer from the building next door to her restaurant showed distinct interest. They'd dated a few times until Richard indicated his desire for a wife. After that she'd kept things light and hadn't slept with him. He bore the bossy gene, a warning to steer clear in her book.

Lana enjoyed her newfound independence too much to step into the marriage trap, yet her body ached for some good, hard, sweaty sex. Right now she thought she might go crazy if she remained celibate for a day longer. The idea of spending one more night aching for the touch, the taste of a man and his hard, hot body covering hers...

A rude snort emerged and Lana decided to get with today's program instead of worrying about her future. A hard run would help ease her tension. She needed to take advantage of her Middlemarch visit since working in New Zealand's adventure capital of Queenstown didn't offer many opportunities for running in feline form.

After a deep breath, Lana pictured a leopard in her mind's eye. She let the change take her, savoring the bite of pain as black fur rippled across her skin. Bones lengthened and popped, sinew stretched and muscles bulged. Her body reshaped and, finally on all fours, she flicked her long tail and padded across the uneven tussock ground.

Scents bombarded her—the spicy hay tang of sun-crisped grasses and the brine of the nearby salt lake, its water evaporated until winter rain and snow refilled it again. She increased her pace to an easy lope, muscles glorying in the motion. Gradually she sprinted, wind whistling across her fur and flattening her whiskers.

A sudden blur of black across her peripheral vision let her know she wasn't alone. Lana snarled and slowed to a walk, baring her teeth at the interloper in warning.

A male.

She sniffed. Go figure. She'd smell different now that her mating mark had vanished. *Available*. Given the shortage of females, the Middlemarch males might consider her fair game. Unlucky for them, she knew every one of their tricks. Her lover—when she chose him—would be human, someone who had no idea of her shapeshifter status and had no intention of trapping her into marriage.

The large black cat who padded up to her ignored her testy mood. Instead he rubbed against her flanks, his low purr of pleasure and contentment bringing an unwilling feline smirk to her mouth. Lana relaxed and whirled without warning. Seconds later, she swatted his nose with her right front paw.

Duncan Ross. The male was younger than her by two years and here to ride in the Middlemarch rodeo. Lana stilled, a thought blooming. Duncan would make the perfect lover despite not being human. They could spend the weekend together, she could satisfy the sexual itch gripping her, and come Monday, Duncan would travel to the next rodeo and his eight seconds of fame while she returned to her life.

The more she pushed and pulled at the idea the better she liked it. They knew each other well since Duncan and Jamie had been cousins. Lana trusted him, knew Duncan never bragged of the women in his life. Her reputation would stay safe.

Duncan barked at her, snagging her attention, and nudged her in the shoulder for good measure. He retreated and sprang at her, wanting to play and wrestle. Ha! He'd have to catch her first.

Grinning, she dodged his charge, whirled and galloped away, darting in and out of the schist outcrops. Her agility and smaller size gave her an advantage. She heard the thump of his paws as he charged after her, his low growl, and her pulse sped, blood thrumming through her veins.

What fun. She loved the thrill of the chase.

Duncan grinned inside as Lana Sinclair darted away with a sexy flick of her tail. A challenge. Hot damn. He'd come to Middlemarch with an express purpose in mind. Lana.

He'd always wanted Lana.

Unfortunately, Jamie had caught and marked her first. He'd loved his cousin as much as he'd desired Lana so he'd stood aside, putting his passion into rodeo instead.

But now...now it was time to make his move.

Lana didn't stand a chance. She might think this a game between friends, but he knew better. The sight of her pretty feline form sparked throbbing need. He quashed the lust spreading through his body, knowing an overt show of sexual desire would scare her away. No, he needed patience. Tender wooing. He'd only have one chance at Lana and knew if he misjudged he'd never have another.

He could not fuck this up.

Duncan raced after her, drawing her musky scent and the underlying vanilla spice deep into his lungs. The feline smirk she aimed over her shoulder brought a rumbling growl deep in his throat. He charged, intent on one thing. The thrill of the chase. She'd think he wanted to play.

This was playtime for adults. If he had his way, there'd be sex in the equation. Lots of sex.

He caught the flick of her tail before she darted behind a pile of gray, weather-beaten rocks and slowed. Given the wind direction, she wouldn't notice him tracking her, and he could take her by surprise. The heat in his body increased, pooling in his loins and making his cock swell. Oh yeah. He wanted Lana, and if he fucked up this courtship, he'd never forgive himself.

Duncan stalked his prey, placing each paw with care, so he didn't give her prior warning. Her scent intensified, and he knew he had her. Once in position, he sprang around the schist, bowling her over until they rolled and tangled in a blur of black fur. He seized the scruff of her neck with his teeth and growled, the sound becoming louder with underlying amusement at her fight for freedom.

Finally, she stilled and her submission almost killed him. All the blood left his head and sank to his cock. He swallowed at scenting the musk of arousal, knowing Lana would detect it too. And wonder. He didn't want her wondering. No. He needed to court her, let her get used to them as a couple then strike. Wham! He'd reel her in before she knew what hit her and they'd be lovers. Partners. Mates.

The prickle of heat from her body and the faint shimmer of light told him she intended to shift back to human. His heart slammed against his ribs and he froze, unsure of how to proceed. Weird. His friends would've ribbed him if they'd witnessed his uncertainty. Yeah, he'd seen her naked before, yet this time seemed different. He'd kept his gaze above her neck, sticking to the social niceties of a group running together.

"Are you going to change?"

Unbidden, his eyes studied her, taking in the small details—her full breasts topped with pink nipples, the narrow waist flaring to curvy hips and lower to study her thighs and sex. Hell. His breath hissed out slowly. She shaved or waxed, leaving smooth skin. His tongue curled inside his mouth as he imagined it rasping across the creamy skin, delving into folds and plunging deep to taste her juices.

"Duncan?"

What the hell was she doing? Stunned, he watched her pluck at one nipple until it stiffened and darkened to a deep rose.

"Duncan, I want you to make love to me. I...I need sex." A faint tide of pink rushed through her cheeks and crawled along her neck to color her chest. "I don't want...just for the weekend," she ended on a rush.

The jolt of lust that speared him made his chest heave while he attempted to breathe through his arousal, tamp it down to acceptable levels. Didn't work. Duncan gave up trying to hide his painful erection and shifted.

"You want what?" She had to tell him again before he'd believe. Surely winning Lana couldn't be this easy?

"I want a lover for the weekend." She captured the plump cushion of her lower lip between her teeth and worried it while avoiding his gaze.

Consternation, fury, jealousy—the whole gambit screwed with his temper. "Do you do this often?" He moved closer, curling his fingers around her biceps until they bit into her tender flesh.

Her gaze flew up to meet his. "No! Of course not. I haven't been with anyone since Jamie."

Duncan relaxed at her impassioned words. *No other man. Good. That was good.* It had been difficult leaving after Jamie's funeral, knowing Lana needed time and he risked another man capturing her interest. Friends and family had kept him in the loop about Lana, not that he'd been upfront regarding his interest.

A month ago gut instinct had told him it was time to return to New Zealand, so he'd come home. Just in time, so it seemed.

He stared at her and detected a smattering of freckles across the bridge of her nose. He'd never noticed them before. Her jade-green eyes tilted up at the corners giving her an exotic look...and her mouth. He'd had serious hard-ons fantasizing about her sexy lower lip, about biting it and laving the nip better, seeing those lips wrapped around his cock.

"Why?" Why him? He wanted to think it was because of his hard abs and charisma, his sex appeal, except his ego wasn't that big. Women didn't normally bowl up to him with a proposition before they'd received the romance, not unless they belonged to the buckle-bunny brigade and wanted to boast of their cowboy conquests.

"Because I don't want to mislead a man into thinking I want something permanent. All I want is no-strings sex." Her chin lifted in faint challenge. "Nothing more."

Duncan frowned, not sure how to react. Part of him simmered with anger at her for going around offering herself. That part wanted to wring her neck. But he also felt flattered and more turned-on than he should be, given the circumstances.

Lana turned away, flashing her rounded arse at him. He caught a hint of feminine pique before she showed him her back. A slow smile curled to life as he stared at the long, slender legs and curvy hips. Yeah, he'd take her up on her offer and play a cat-and-mouse game. Her offer made things easy for him, but if she thought he'd walk away after a weekend, the woman had rocks in her head. He wanted to retire from the rodeo circuit, settle down and breed bucking bulls.

No, Lana belonged to him—she just didn't know it yet.

Duncan's erection looked huge, his desire difficult to miss, so why wasn't he accepting her offer? Most men would jump at the chance of sex with no conditions attached. Her forehead furrowed in confusion, a smidge of irritation. Bother the man. She hadn't remembered him being so...so...male. True, she hadn't seen him for two years. Her memory couldn't be that faulty?

"I'm sorry if I embarrassed you," she said, turning away. "I'll go."

"You haven't embarrassed me." He grasped her forearm to halt her departure, his warm breath wafting across the shell of her ear. The gentle yet determined grip on her shoulders forced her to face him. His cock brushed her stomach when he drew her closer. A shiver worked through her at the contact and her body softened, moistened at the thought of sex with Duncan. Desire kicked in her belly. Oh, she was glad she'd seen Duncan and thought of him to fill the lover position. Now if only he'd take action.

"If I haven't embarrassed or offended you, then why are you stalling?"

He chuckled, a dark and arousing sound that drifted goose bumps over her arms and legs. "Why haven't I pounced?"

Lana peeked at his erection and flicked her tongue over her lips in a provocative manner. Anything to prod the stubborn male to pass go, collect his bounty. She hadn't thought she'd experience difficulty in finding a willing lover. Weren't men easy anymore? "Yeah. Is there something wrong with me?"

"Not a thing, sweetheart. Not a thing."

Her brows arched, and she fought to keep her tetchiness at bay. "Well?"

"Sometimes a man likes to do the chasing. It's part of the cat-and-mouse game."

"I am *not* a mouse."

Humor flashed in his dark green eyes. "No, you're a beautiful kitty."

Indignation rose. "I'm not—" His kiss cut off the rest of the sentence. Masterful. Assured. He took over. Her irritation dispersed at the first touch and she leaned into his larger frame, curling her hands around his neck to anchor her during the storm. Her fingers crept into his black hair, noting the soft downiness and his rich green scent, fresh and masculine. He nibbled and licked her lips, teasing and pushing past every defense until all she could do was feel, become a creature of sensation. A primitive throb filled her veins, and she melted under his expertise.

One of his hands lowered to cup her butt, the calluses on his long fingers rasping across her tender skin. She shivered, groaned and opened her mouth to him. So hot. She wondered if she'd burn alive but couldn't stop, didn't want to halt. Flames licked through her body with each sweet stroke of his tongue into her mouth.

He lifted his head, and she moaned a soft complaint, words of protest forming on her lips, when he stepped back, releasing her from his grasp. The heat in his eyes stilled any objection. His gaze stroked like a physical touch as it ran across her shoulders, her collarbone and finally her breasts. She gnawed at her bottom lip to control her moan. No matter how much she wanted sex, she didn't want to give Duncan ideas of how bad she craved release with a man, her desperation. Knowledge gave him power, and that would never do.

"Touch me," she pleaded. "Please touch me."

With his gaze holding hers, he reached out, taking one pouting pink nipple between finger and thumb. He twisted it hard, which should have hurt. Instead, a gossamer ribbon of pleasure shot to her pussy. She sucked in an excited breath, sensing the lovemaking would feel good, everything she needed to satiate the sexual urges thrumming through her veins.

"Now," she said. "Take me."

Duncan hesitated. She knew he wanted her—his erection told her that, yet the stubborn man still dithered, as if he thought he knew better. Rot. Two years extra experience at living gave her more insight. *Seize the day*. Duncan had to grab the opportunities coming his way, not develop a conscience and dawdle.

Temper loosened her tongue, and she issued a challenge. "If you don't take me, I intend to go to the rodeo dance tonight and pick someone else. I want to fuck. I want to fuck *now*."

"Be careful what you ask for, Lana." A hint of steel crept into his lazy voice.

"I'm tired of people telling me what to do, how to act. I didn't die when Jamie did." Lana spun away, pictured the leopard in her mind and smoothly shifted. Then she ran. She raced away without looking back, frustrated and angry and tearful all at once. It wasn't meant to happen like this. Why couldn't Duncan just take what she offered without making things complicated?

The wind whistled across her fur, muscles bunched and lengthened with her ground-eating lope, and all she heard was the frenzied thoughts zapping through her head. He didn't want her. She'd made a fool of herself. And even worse, she'd have to go to the stupid rodeo dance and make good on her threat.

Lana heard the thunder of paws seconds before Duncan pounced. With his larger, more muscular body, he herded her into a dip sheltered from the wind by a pile of schist and several sprawling, scrubby trees. When she tried to move, he nipped her on the shoulder, sharp teeth digging into her flesh. Lana whirled, her lips curling up in a snarl. How dare he attempt to handle her? Dominate?

Inside a frisson of pleasure shot through her, one she didn't take time to decipher. Instead she shook herself free and snarled again for good measure, her ears flattening against her head. Dammit, he couldn't treat her this way. She drew away, muscles gathering to spring to freedom if he gave her the opportunity. Her tail flicked in annoyance. She darted to the right.

He headed her off, herding her against the rocks. When she glanced in the opposite direction, he growled long and low. Mean. Lana froze in indecision. Surely he wouldn't hurt her?

Duncan backed up, watchful and wary as he studied her. When she didn't move again, he morphed to human. "Shift," he barked.

Lana hesitated, taking in the taut stance, the determined set to his mouth. Nerves fluttered in her stomach, underscored by a strange excitement.

"Now, Lana."

Lana obeyed and seconds later stood in front of him. "What?" Her shoulder stung where he'd bitten her and she pressed the fingers of one hand to the aching spot.

"You said you wanted sex."

"I've changed my mind."

He prowled closer. "Too late," he growled, his heavy erection swinging enough to snare her attention. "I'm accepting."

Before she could move, he pinned her against the rocks.

"Hands above your head. Now," he snapped. "Do it."

Bemused, she obeyed, leaning into the warm rock. She placed her hands above her head. The move lifted her breasts, bringing to mind a sexual offering. She swallowed at the gleam in his eyes, her tongue darting out to moisten dry lips. Something had shifted between them. It wasn't the kiss. Something else. Suddenly she became ultra aware of her body, his body and the entire male-female thing.

Duncan trailed a finger across her collarbone, sensitizing her skin with the callused drag until it burned like a brand. A throb started at the juncture of her thighs and she shifted her weight. With an inward sigh, she gave in to the need to stroke and lowered her hands. He stopped touching her, stepping back to glower.

"I'm not going further until your hands are above your head."

She glared, but he remained implacable. With bad grace she obeyed and his fingers trailed across the top curve of one breast. His finger circled the areola, leaving a trail of prickly sensation in its wake. At her sharp inhalation, he met her gaze. The heat and silent messages conveyed in that one glance bombarded her brain with lustful messages while her pussy creamed for him. God, she'd never guessed he'd be this intense.

He bent his head and the slow slide of his tongue followed the path his finger had traveled. Lana quivered, her knees trembling under the sensual attack. Despite her lingering pique at his overbearing behavior, she craved more. The need, the desire after months alone demanded release. Begging words crammed her throat when he continued to tease instead of moving to a satisfactory conclusion. Finally, her desperation spilled free.

"Please. *Please do something*."

"Say my name."

"Duncan, please. Please don't tease me."

"Tell me what you want."

Hadn't she made it obvious? She stared at him in bemusement. Defiance. Her pussy fluttered and a deep-seated ache fired between her legs. Lana squeezed her thighs together to assuage the sensual throb. The move made the ache worse, made her realize how wet she was for him, how much she craved his body.

"Tell me," he growled.

"I want you."

"Do you want my finger? My mouth? Give me details."

Lana moaned low and throaty at the thought of his blunt finger invading her channel, pushing against the slick walls of her sex. Stretching her.

"Yes," she whispered, heat suffusing her body, pulling her nipples to tight points. She transferred her weight from foot to foot, the pervasive ache in her pussy driving her crazy. Maybe she shouldn't rub her legs together? Lana widened her stance and moaned at the cool air brushing her swollen folds. It didn't feel better. The ache had intensified.

Duncan leaned closer, his breath a warm puff against her ear when he spoke. "Just my finger, Lana? Is that all you want?"

Unbidden, she glanced at his erection. It was thick and pointed outward, blue veins visible beneath the surface. The head appeared swollen, a deep red, and as she watched, a pearl of liquid formed at the slit. She swallowed. "I want your cock."

He nodded in a thoughtful manner as if considering her request. Lana attempted to swallow and realized stress had formed a lump in her throat. Tension pulsed to life, tightening her muscles, almost replacing her sexual desire.

Duncan moved lazily, stepping back, so he didn't crowd her anymore. He dropped one hand to cup his erection. The air hissed out of her and she couldn't help but watch. With a leisurely pull, he stroked his cock while watching her the entire time. He clearly enjoyed the touch and didn't mind the audience, she thought, miffed at his exhibition. She wondered what he wanted to prove. That he could get himself off by masturbating? Newsflash—any fool could do that. The end result left one feeling empty and unsatisfied.

He kept the strokes slow and even, his slit weeping as he fisted his shaft. "How do you want my cock? Inside that luscious mouth of yours? Or maybe inside your sweet little cunt?"

Lana's mouth dropped open in shock. She had never...no one had ever spoken to her in this manner before. She wanted to tell him she was a lady. *Big, fat lie.* She couldn't deny the rush of arousal in reaction to his words and propositioning him wasn't a ladylike action.

While she watched, he pulled on his cock again and stroked a thumb over the head, sweeping away the liquid. Seconds later, another bead glistened at the slit.

"Or maybe you'd like my cock in your arse, Lana?"

She gasped, the throb in her pussy intensifying to downright painful. It seemed dirty talk turned her on, flipped her switches and took her from zero to ready-to-go in seconds flat.

"What do you say, Lana?" Duncan's eyes glittered, a dark jade green, his gaze intense and unrelenting. "How do you want me?"

Lana clenched her muscles, excitement and trepidation warring inside her. She hoped it didn't show on her face. "You...you decide. I don't mind."

"But what if I decide on something kinky, Lana?" He eyed her closely, his large body tense.

Oh heck. "How kinky?" Her question emerged with a squeak, and her stomach hollowed with the sharp whip of erotic fear. What had she set in motion?

Chapter 2

Seduction

D uncan wanted to laugh at the panic dancing across her expressive face. It wasn't nice of him to tease her, but he didn't want Lana to think him easy. She would not wrap him around her little finger and make a yes-man out of him. *No*. Right from the start he needed her to know he enjoyed sex. He liked to do things his way and dominate in the bedroom. Outside the bedroom he wanted a partnership, but he'd learned enough about himself to admit he couldn't tolerate anything except sweet submission in the sexual arena.

He wasn't a traditional guy. That frightened some women. His gut told him Lana would handle him, his needs, just fine.

She licked her lips and sneaked a glance at his cock. A longing gaze. Oh yeah. Lana Sinclair would enjoy what he offered, and by the end of the weekend she'd crave him enough to keep him around. Cat and mouse. Confidence filled him when he caught yet another furtive peek. *Good girl. Let's give you a hint of pleasure and reel you in.*

"We'll start slow." Duncan almost laughed at her palpable relief. "No, leave your hands where they are."

"They're sore."

"Just a little longer, sweetheart. Do it for me." He noticed the subtle tremor of her arms, her uncomfortable fidgeting, and wanted to push her, take her farther than she'd gone before.

She nodded, the acknowledgment lacking confidence. Duncan knew that would change. She'd learn how much pleasure awaited, how good it could be for both of them if she trusted him. He dipped his head to take one taut pink nipple into his mouth. He tongued it, forcing the bud against his teeth to give her an extra edge of sensation. Her soft cry and the tight grip of her hands burrowing into his hair brought an inward grin. Despite her disobedience, he couldn't find it in him to discipline her for flouting his rules. Not yet. The sweet taste of her skin and the spicy honey scent of her pushed him to hurry. He sank to his knees and gripped her thighs.

"Duncan?"

"Shush," he soothed. "Part your legs for me. Yeah. That's it." A burst of her spicy scent engulfed him. He panted, trying to tamp down his excitement. Knowing he would take her, fuck her soon, had his cock weeping, his balls so tight he feared bursting.

Concentrate, he scolded himself. *Get Lana off first, then you can take her while her pretty pussy is still pulsing from climax.*

He stroked his fingers across the tender skin of her inner thighs, gloried in her sharp intake of breath. This close her feminine scent enticed him and he imagined how sweet she'd taste on his tongue. With his lips he nuzzled the baby-soft skin of her mound and licked a wet path along the crease between leg and pelvis. He parted her pink folds, felt her searing heat seconds before he raked his tongue along her cleft. He grinned at her hungry whimper. Good, and far better than anything his imagination could conjure. She trembled at the skim of his tongue across her clit, and her fevered moan warned him of her tenuous control. Not much better than his. Time for action. He upped the erotic assault and pushed one finger into her, groaning aloud at the wet, silken heat. Her breathing hitched, and another tremor ripped through her body.

His patience at an end, Duncan pulled his finger free and scooped her into his arms. Ignoring her startled yelp, he placed her in a part of the sheltered hollow where the tussock grass grew thick. Hardly the perfect place for seduction. At this stage he didn't care. For a long second he raked his gaze over her curvy form, letting it settle on the deep pink flesh between her splayed legs. The sun glinted off her juices while Lana watched him with big, wide eyes.

"You ready?"

"Yes! That's what I've been trying to tell—"

Lana watched him as he moved over her, predatory intent written on his face and highlighted by the sexual flush on his cheekbones. His hands dropped to cup her buttocks, he positioned himself at her entrance and penetrated her with a powerful thrust. Overwhelming sensations fizzled through her, heart thundering at the invasion of his thick cock. Nothing hurt. Instead she felt full and stretched, almost beyond comfort.

The sensations—the weight of his body and the flicker of pleasure rippling from her swollen clit sated some of her impatience. Her eyes fluttered shut to concentrate on the unbearable pleasure of his possession. This, she had missed so much.

Greedy, she ran her hands over his smooth back and lower to cup his buttocks, encouraging him to move. She dug her fingernails into the tight muscles and undulated beneath him in clear demand.

He chuckled. "Lucky for you, sweetheart, my control is almost shot."

Before she could puzzle over his remark, he thrust. At first they were slow and even strokes. His mouth covered hers and she tasted his hunger along with the musk from her own body. The tang of arousal drifted around them, combining with the earthy flavors of the outdoors. Suddenly he grasped her hands and lifted them above her head, manacling them together using one hand. Then, he ground into her with hard digs of his cock, the frenzied plunges leaving her in no doubt of his sexual appetite.

Enjoyment swirled in her, mysterious and fleeting. He wasn't hitting her in the right spot. Desperate, she angled her hips, arching and letting out a fevered cry when she achieved the perfect alignment. The ripples of pleasure started, her pussy clutching at his shaft, pulsing in small tremors, desire consuming her.

"Good. So good," she whispered.

"I know."

If anything his cock grew larger, the tight fit unbearably perfect. He snarled, his face contorted in a primeval mask, and the tension in her burst as she exploded with painful pleasure. She was dimly aware of his guttural shout. Deep shudders shook his frame and his seed jetted from him in powerful spurts. The storm quieted, and they lay entwined, still connected.

Duncan released her wrists and pulled his weight off her, turning their bodies so they lay on their sides. "You okay?"

Okay? *Okay?* Did a puddle-like feeling rate as okay? Her eyes opened to his scrutiny. "So good." Her pussy contracted in a spasm around his cock, making her realize he still filled her with his hard length.

"I didn't hurt you?" Faint worry showed in the slight creases on his forehead.

"No, why would you hurt me?" She wrinkled her nose, feeling relaxed and replete. "My only complaint is your pace. I could have come like that half an hour ago."

Duncan shook his head. "Complaints. You're lucky I'm not near my ropes. I'd tie you up and punish you for failing to obey my instructions."

"What sort of punishment?"

Working hard to suppress his grin, he ran his hand over her bottom. Full and curvy, the skin soft and creamy, her fine backside fulfilled his dreams. Damn, he could still remember his first sight of her wearing tight blue jeans. About to make a move until Jamie had walked up to her and slung his arm around her shoulders in clear ownership, he'd choked back his instincts and played the friend card. This arse was now his to touch and play with. After separating their bodies, he bent his head and took a bite.

"Ow! If you're hungry, chase a rabbit."

"I'm hungry all right, but first there's a little matter of disobedience." He pushed her flat on her stomach, cupping his hand around one buttock before lifting it and giving her a sharp smack. She jumped. He held her in place with his hand in the small of her back. The pink imprint of his palm brought intense satisfaction. His. He smacked her again, the sharp crack making the blow sound harder than it was.

She wriggled, trying to evade his touch. "Enough! I'm not a naughty child."

"No, you're a very sexy woman who won't obey even when my instructions are given to enhance pleasure."

A snort emerged and, grinning, he brought his hand down for a third time, admiring the fiery blush and the contrast to the rest of her pale skin.

"Why is this making me hot?" she muttered in an undertone, obviously talking to herself.

"You like that?"

"Yes. No! That was a private conversation with myself. I don't enjoy having my bottom tapped like a naughty girl."

It sure as hell made him hot and ready to fuck her again. "Part your legs for me. Let me see how wet you are. Yeah. Just like that. Perfect." Duncan stroked his finger across her labia, spreading the wet, swollen folds. He bent to blow a stream of warm air on her slit, closely attuning to her reactions because he wanted to learn what made her hot.

"Do I get a turn being boss?"

"Nope. You asked for a weekend and I said yes, but on my terms."

"Bully. Are you going to let me up?"

"We haven't finished yet, kitty. Not by a long shot."

"Don't call me kitty. I hate it."

Duncan grinned again, aware he'd had more fun today than he'd had in a long time, not that he'd suffered from lack of female attention. Women adored cowboys and weren't shy about letting him know. He wouldn't be male if he hadn't indulged in carefree fun. Sharp desire rippled through him to settle in his balls. "Push up on all fours for me. I want to fuck you from behind. After I color your sweet arse some more."

Lana trembled, obeying him, lifting to her hands and knees. His cock bucked, his balls drawing tight. This time he intended to pace himself. He smacked her lower, so the sting ran across her sex. After another smack he noticed she lifted so the flat of his hand struck in the same place. He parted the globes of her ass and trailed a finger across her rosette. She started, body tensing. He repeated the move while he slid two fingers into her sodden pussy. Her soft groan made his shaft buck, the curving glans sliding across her hip.

"Duncan."

She said his name so sweetly and with such longing he strummed his thumb along her cleft, skimming the edge of her clit to give her a hint of sensation. He curved his fingers inside, seeking her sweet spot while he continued to tease her hard nub. Each move of his thumb came closer until she strained beneath him, moaning when he massaged her internally.

A shudder racked her body, and he increased his assault, determined to give her pleasure. By the end of the weekend she wouldn't be able to look at him without thinking of sex and the thick slice of pleasure he offered with each touch. If he showed her how good they could be together, she might come to believe there was only one alternative for them.

"I don't think torture is meant to feel this good."

"Only good. I must be doing something wrong." His cock throbbed at the spurt of juices in her tight pussy. He massaged, bending his head to nibble the glowing skin of her buttocks. With a groan that came close to a wail she came, channel squeezing his fingers while the scrape of his teeth brought a violent flutter. Her hands gave out, her forearms dropping to the ground while her pussy still grabbed at his fingers. Hell, she was hot.

"Nothing a little practice wouldn't hurt," she muttered.

Duncan smirked. Practice he could do. He removed his hands, and she turned to face him, her hair in wild disarray, her eyes sparkling. Absently, he sucked his fingers clean while he stared at her pretty face. *His.* The word kept echoing through his mind in an endless litany.

"Up on your hands and knees again."

A furrow formed on her brow. "Why?"

"Because I want to take you from behind." And because his feline was riding him hard, simmering below the surface and threatening to take over, marking his territory before he'd romanced Lana to his way of thinking.

She frowned, suspecting something, but Duncan maintained his easygoing expression, letting a hint of humor shine through and leering at her breasts. Anything to lull her suspicions.

Without haste, she resumed her former position and Duncan's breath eased out in a whoosh of relief.

Giving in to temptation, he moved behind her and reached out to cup one breast before rolling the nipple between finger and thumb. "You have pretty breasts, sweetheart."

"Thanks," she whispered. "Duncan, I've missed this so much."

A shard of jealousy pierced his sexual hunger. Jamie. His cousin had died and yet Duncan envied him. "No problem. We're friends. I'd do anything for you." Fuck, he had to change the subject, get things back to a strictly sexual nature before he said the wrong thing. He tugged her nipple, pulling a ragged sigh from her. The soft cry went straight to his cock, coalescing in a throb. Hell, that sound. He wanted to hear more of her breathy moans.

"You ready for me?" He could see the glaze of arousal on her inner thighs and couldn't resist the quick plunge of fingers into her tight channel. *Oh yeah. Perfect.*

"Yesterday," she muttered, her tone cross. "I wanted sex yesterday."

Little did she know. Pulling his fingers free, he lined up his cock and pushed his tip inside her. Heat struck him in an intense burst. Part of him wanted to slam into her. He resisted, thrusting in measured strokes and pulling back before pushing into her scalding heat a bit farther. Finally, fully seated, and he paused, leaning over to nuzzle her neck. The scent of sex flowed around them, and a faint floral perfume came from her hair. He licked a path from below her ear right down to her collarbone, enjoying the flavor of her skin and the vanilla spice scent of it.

"Stop dawdling."

"My way," he reminded her.

Lana growled, pulling her hips forward and slamming back to make his cock slide through her channel. He hissed, his nerve endings vibrating inside her wet depths.

"Hold still." Not trusting her to follow his orders, he grasped her hips and held her tight. He leaned over her again, brushing his chest against her spine, sliding his lips across the smooth vulnerability of her throat. A nip of his teeth made her jump and a quick punch of heat hit him along with masculine satisfaction. *His*.

Lana clenched her inner muscles, tightening her sheath around his dick. He groaned, the sound almost drowning out her victorious laugh.

"A pity our first time is out here," he said, warning coloring his words.

Another laugh preceded the clenching of her inner muscles. "You can't control everything."

And he'd thought she'd follow along with his instructions. Hell, he'd underestimated her. It had been a while since someone had defied him in the same way as Lana. Damned if it didn't make the sex better.

"Duncan, stop dithering. I feel like one big throb. I need you to move."

A grin slipped free. The female didn't know when to stop. What he needed was a distraction so she stopped issuing orders and complaints. Still smiling, he withdrew before gliding back into her moist heat. A groan built in his chest but he held it back, determined to gain the upper hand in this battle of wills. He licked a path up her spine, over the tiny bumps and indentations, his pulse speeding once his mouth neared the juncture of her shoulder and neck. *Jesus*. The urge to bite, to mark her shoved at his control. He shuddered and forced himself to pull away, to pull out of her sweet pussy until only his tip rested inside.

"Duncan."

With a growl, he ignored the protest and pounded into her. Hard. Fast. Using more force than usual because he knew Lana could take it rough. Hah! *Not the truth*. The minx had pushed past his shaky control. He slammed into her again, lips curving. At least she'd ceased her complaints. Good.

The way to obedience lay in hot sex. Couldn't be better.

Wouldn't last much longer. He slipped a hand between her legs and rubbed her clit. She gasped, her pussy gripping his cock in a tight kiss of pleasure. Man, he'd never expected this from Lana. His fingers massaged the slippery nub again. Good sex, yeah—but not spectacular and mind-blowing. The finding firmed his plans.

Him. Lana. A mated pair.

There was no other alternative.

Another brush of his fingers and he felt her topple into climax. He thrust in hard digs, the kiss of her channel firing off more pleasure than he'd ever experienced. A guttural groan forced past sharp canine teeth.

Hell. A glance at his hands confirmed it. He'd started his change. Fuck. Even his damned cock wanted in on the action, both lengthening and widening to fill her completely. Hoping to distract her, he rasped his tongue over her shoulder and pulled back, thrusting rapidly to finish.

"Duncan." This time his name exited on a sigh of feminine pleasure.

Better. Much better. Filing the info away for the future, he sank into her wet pussy, soft tissues gripping and massaging his dick. His balls had drawn up tight, the tingle of orgasm firing along the length of his cock. He groaned, loving the sounds of fucking, her scent. Seeing his honey-coated cock shoving into her body. Another hard plunge into her clinging pussy and orgasm thundered through him. Blind with pleasure, he gripped her hips, each breath a harsh rasp. When the jets of semen ceased, he pulled out of her, lifting and turning her into his arms.

Like a sleepy kitten, she cuddled into him, pressing her head against his chest. Right where she should be, he thought in satisfaction.

Belatedly he realized they hadn't used contraception. No problem on the disease front, however, pregnancy was always a possibility. He thought about raising the topic and dismissed it, not wanting to draw the hellcat to the surface. Plenty of time for talking later, besides, the idea of a kid didn't bother him. He held her close, let the breeze drift her long hair across his arm and breathed in the scent of her, a combination of the fresh outdoors and a sexy musk that made his nostrils quiver, his arms tighten around her. Duncan listened to her low breathing and hoped things would settle between them. He wanted to spend the rest of his life holding her, listening to the steady rhythm of her inhalations and smelling her beautiful scent.

Lana stirred, her eyes opening a fraction, dark lashes screening her expression. She stiffened in his arms, which pissed him off. Not that he displayed any of his reaction. Instead he relaxed his grip and let her pull away enough so he could kiss her. Their lips met, a gentle brushing of mouths. He'd intended to soothe her. Comfort. Instead a jolt of sexual pleasure assaulted him. And her soft gasp told him he wasn't alone. He wanted to love her again.

"Where are you staying?"

"With Emily and Saber Mitchell. Emily invited me."

Duncan frowned. A motel room might have been easier. Maybe if he had a quiet word with Saber.

"What about you?"

"Camping at the rodeo grounds." And he wasn't about to take her in his tent where everyone else could hear her cries of pleasure. He didn't care if his mates ribbed him, but he refused to let her reputation suffer. "I haven't seen Saber for a while. Are you heading back there now?"

"Yes."

Duncan stared, his gaze zeroing in on her plump lips and the way she worried them with her teeth. God, if the woman didn't stop nibbling on her bottom lip, he wouldn't be responsible for his actions.

"Good. I'll come with you," he said.

"But—"

Duncan stood, took pleasure in the furtive way she eyed him up and down before accepting the hand he offered.

"You don't need to escort me back to the Mitchells."

"Do I embarrass you?"

"No. No, of course not."

His eyes narrowed at her refusal to look at him. She didn't want anyone to know they'd slept together. Frustration ate at his gut. Damn. He didn't intend to be anyone's guilty secret.

"Relax. My mother taught me manners." Not much else before she left him with relations and headed out with a man, but that had nothing to do with them. "I'm not about to embarrass you or do anything to hurt your reputation. Are you going to the dance tonight?"

"Yes, with Emily and Saber."

"Save a dance for me?"

This time she frowned. "I thought you were walking me home."

"Sure thing." Ah, sex and keeping her off balance. Worked like a charm.

Chapter 3

The Dance

Lana couldn't take her gaze off Duncan. He strode across the tussock at her side, dressed in faded jeans, a long-sleeved blue shirt rolled up to reveal tanned forearms and scuffed boots. The man prowled with catlike grace, his dark hair too long, long enough to curl at his nape. He stood taller than her, lean and muscular. Not as big as Jamie but all man. Experienced man. Her muscles sang with a few achy parts, a reminder of the pleasure they'd shared.

Duncan plucked a stalk of dried grass. "How long since you've visited Middlemarch?"

"I think the last time I visited was for Saber and Emily's wedding."

"I wish I'd been able to make the wedding."

Curiosity simmered in Lana. "Why did you come home? Emily told me you're doing well on the rodeo circuit in the States."

"I missed home." He turned to her, their gazes locking.

Lana's breath caught in her throat and a bolt of sensation spiraled through her body. This was about scratching an itch. Sex and nothing more.

Duncan shrugged. "I might go back once the season finishes here."

An ocean between them might work. A few inches sure as hell wasn't doing much to halt the impulse to touch. Damn, she couldn't believe how much she craved him. It wasn't right. It wasn't natural. She didn't want another man underfoot, always telling her what to do and when, expecting her to pop out children instead of following her career. Cooking was all she knew and something she loved. Lana knew she excelled at it. Her restaurant continued to boom. She didn't need a man. When it came to children, Jamie hadn't agreed on the timing. Oh, Jamie had loved her, but the lack of children had played on his mind. A lot.

She should leave and go back to Queenstown early. She'd had sex. Pleasurable, sensational sex. Yeah, she felt sated, except along with physical satisfaction came edginess. Awareness. And a scary yearning for more. The worst freaking part.

"I hear voices out the back," Duncan said when they neared the front door of the Mitchell homestead.

They circled the house, taking the flower-edged path leading to the rear of the property. A cobblestone barbeque area extended from the wall of the kitchen. To their right a thriving vegetable garden gave way to an expanse of green lawn, the tall trees surrounding and shading the property. It seemed like an oasis at the height of the Otago summer.

"Good run?" Emily took in Duncan and smiled, her eyes crinkling at the edges. She waved at the empty seat beside her. "Saber is in the kitchen getting drinks. Why don't you go and say hello?" she said to Duncan.

Duncan bent to brush a kiss on Emily's cheek.

Jealousy, swift and cutting, seared through Lana bringing a follow-up wave of shock. Emily appeared happily married to Saber. She wasn't interested in Duncan. He disappeared through the door leading to the kitchen and her eyes zoomed in on his butt.

"Do I detect a romance?"

Lana ripped her gaze away and bolted upright. "Heck no!" At Emily's look of disbelief, she blushed. "It's just sex. Just for the weekend."

"Hmm." Emily's brows rose in clear disbelief. "Was it good?"

"Yes, and that's all you're getting from me. I don't ask you about your sex life."

Emily chuckled. "You work hard, Lana, and deserve fun." She paused a beat. "So are you still staying the night or are you spending it with Duncan?"

"I'm staying here." Lana attempted not to flush at the teasing. Emily had an advantage over her, honing her skills on her brothers-in-law.

"Okay. I'll tell Saber if we hear someone sneaking around in the middle of the night we shouldn't worry because it will be

Duncan. Heck, I know. We'll leave the door unlocked. He can walk right inside. Neither of you are getting any younger. You shouldn't have to do acrobatics just to scratch an itch."

"Emily!"

"What's she been up to now?" Saber asked, strolling outside with a tray of drinks, looking cool and sexy in a T-shirt and shorts. Duncan was right behind him, and judging by his grin, they'd both heard everything. Saber handed both women a glass of wine before the two men dropped into empty wooden seats.

"She's just being Emily," Lana said with a glower at her grinning friend. "And I'm not listening to a word she says." Saber and Emily were a great couple. She'd known Saber all her life and had met Emily at the wedding. They'd hit it off because they were both chefs running their own businesses and had so much in common. Emily had a café in Middlemarch called Storm in a Teacup. They spoke to each other regularly by phone and met whenever the couple visited Queenstown.

"I keep threatening to beat her," Saber said. "Threats don't work so I've given up."

Emily snorted. "He's just glad I'm picking on someone else instead of him."

Saber winked at Lana and didn't deny his wife's accusation. "Emily said you went for a run."

Lana glanced at Duncan, saw his heated look and blushed. "Um, yes," she managed.

"She doesn't want to discuss it," Emily said. "That topic got me into trouble."

Duncan chuckled, grinned at Emily and edged the conversation into rodeo. A relief to Lana.

"How are you doing in the standings this year?" Saber asked.

"Third in the bull riding," Duncan said. "I stuck to the one category this season, and I missed two rodeos before I arrived back from the States. You both heading to the dance tonight?"

"Sure are," Emily said. "I'm looking forward to it." She glanced at Saber. "I missed most of the last dance they had. His fault. Lana's going too, but you already know that."

"Emily," Lana protested, off balance despite laughing along with the others. Just the weekend. After the rodeo she'd head back to Queenstown.

Country and Western music poured from the huge marquee along with laughter, some of it with a tinge of alcohol-induced hilarity, filled the air by the time Duncan and three other cowboys wandered over from the campsite. Determination rode him because he knew he'd have a fight on his hands to get close to Lana. Even though tonight wasn't the main event, there were still many people gathered at the party to raise funds for the local fire service who also carried out search and rescue in the area. The local men, the visiting cowboys and the woman herself would impede his goal. Too bad. He'd waited a long time and wasn't about to back off without a fight.

The local committee had gone all out with decorations, including Wanted posters and a display of Western memorabilia just inside the entrance. He paid his admission and sauntered into the marquee, looking for Lana or either of the Mitchells. Difficult to scent anyone in this crowd. Men and women packed the dance floor, attempting to do a line dance.

Damn. He couldn't see Lana. With a soft curse, he pushed his way through the crowd, pausing here and there to say hello to friends and acquaintances. Along with his unease came a contrasting sense of contentment. It was damned fine being home, spending time with his fellow shifters.

"Are you looking for me?" The throaty voice dragged his attention from the dance floor.

Jesus, she looked beautiful. She wore a dark green dress with tiny straps to hold it up. It clung to her curves before falling to swish in loose folds around her knees. The color highlighted her eyes, deepening jade green to a darker, more mysterious hue. The shadow of her cleavage drew his attention. He took half a step toward her before halting. Not the time or place. The closest he'd get to touching during the next few hours would be a slow dance, or if he could persuade her to take a walk with him outside where the air was cool and privacy easier to find.

"Yeah. I thought you might be dancing." But glad he didn't have to see another man touch her.

She stood on tiptoe and kissed him on the lips, a brief brush on the mouth that had his feline purring. "I have been dancing. I saw you come in and wanted to say hello."

The line dance ended, and the band rolled into a slow dance. Perfect.

"Wanna dance with me?"

"Sure."

They walked over to the makeshift dance floor and she slipped into his arms where she belonged. Her arms stretched up to grip his shoulders and their bodies brushed.

"You look beautiful." Nothing less than the truth. The full skirt of her dress flirted with the tops of her knees, stirring with each gliding step. He would have preferred that she wear a sack, just so none of the other men could ogle her sexy form. Unfortunately, he could hardly complain since the other women had dressed in a similar manner. He wondered how long it'd take to talk her out of that dress, pondered again the advisability of taking a walk.

"Thanks. You look pretty good yourself."

They danced in silence for a while, Duncan content to hold her in his arms. One dance flowed into another.

"This is nice. I never have a chance to dance."

He grunted an affirmative reply. That would make him a bastard if he asked her to take a walk. Fuck. Okay. He'd steer her into the far corner where some enterprising cowboys had dimmed the lights. Yeah. Sounded like a plan. He danced her across the floor, navigating dancers, cuddling her close and reveling in the softness of her body brushing his, her enticing scent of vanilla and the crisp outdoors.

The song ended and he stepped away from her. "Want a drink?"

"Sure. Emily and Saber are over in the corner. Do you want to sit with them?"

"Do you want wine?" Damn, the woman ate him up with her eyes. She shouldn't do that—not if she knew what was good for her.

Lana winked, her dark lashes sweeping over her cheeks in a sexy fan. "Perfect." His gaze drifted to her soft, glistening lips. Appealing and sensual. He fought the urge to dip his head and claim her mouth.

"Sit with Emily and I'll bring over the drinks." He started for the bar before stopping and turning back. "Lana, don't dance with anyone else."

"But that wouldn't be polite."

"Fuck polite. You offered me the weekend." Duncan strode off to the bar, urgency simmering through his veins. The bloody woman made him crazy. He recalled their lovemaking, the sensation of burying his cock deep in her hot pussy and now he craved a repeat. Once with Lana wasn't enough.

Duncan waited his turn at the bar, speaking to one of the elders and a girl he'd gone to school with. Spotting Saber with the two women, he ordered a beer for him.

When he arrived at the table Lana sat on her own.

She leaned close so he could hear over the music. "Saber and Emily are dancing. They'll be back soon."

He nodded, handing her a glass of wine while debating a walk. Bugger it. The weekend was too short for pussyfooting around. "Would you like to go for a walk?"

"In here?"

His brows rose.

"Oh," she said, laughing. "I guess you meant outside."

"Yeah."

"We should wait for Emily and Saber to come back so they don't lose their table."

Yes! "Yeah, okay." He picked up his beer and took a sip. Damn, he was shaking. He counted to ten to distract himself from thoughts of sex, and in particular, sex with Lana. Didn't work. His cock stirred, bucking like a bull coming out of the chute. He glanced at the dance floor then at the band, willing them to finish.

It was a long five minutes until he spotted Saber and Emily.

"Have you finished your drink?"

Lana tilted her head, her long, dark hair slipping over one cheekbone. "Are you in a hurry?"

"Damn straight."

She blinked before her sexy lips curved into a smile. "Let's go for that walk then."

"We're going for a walk," he said to Saber in a terse voice, not bothering to wait for a reply.

Yeah, baby. The wicked glint in Lana's eyes pulled his dick even tighter. He stood and held out his hand, not letting her go even when one of his friends stopped him to talk about tomorrow's rodeo.

"Gotta go, Kev. We're meeting someone." He didn't wait for a reply this time either, instead dragging Lana from the marquee, marching away from the noise and gaiety of the fundraiser.

"Where are we going?"

"Somewhere private," Duncan said.

"Is it necessary to run?"

Duncan slowed, letting Lana catch up. Her heels sank into the grass and she yanked them out with a trace of impatience. A frown tightened her luscious lips.

"And do we have to go cross country?"

He stepped up close and kissed her, sliding their lips together until the tightness left her body. She softened, leaning into him, rubbing her breasts against his chest. No bra.

"Lana." He dipped his fingers beneath the curved neckline of her dress, peeling one narrow strap off her shoulder. His mouth followed the path of his fingers, taking tiny nibbles of her silky skin.

"Oops! Sorry. Didn't mean to interrupt."

Duncan didn't see who the man was who'd spoken since he beat a fast retreat.

"Come on." Duncan scooped her off her feet and carried her rapidly along a dirt path and out of the light into a stand of trees. By the time he stopped walking the sounds of revelry were much farther away. He set her down in the deep shadows. "It should be more private here."

"Kiss me."

"I intend to." And a lot more. He lowered his head to claim her lips, pushing his tongue inside. A hint of crisp wine danced across his receptors as he devoured her mouth, and he gloried in her moan of pleasure. It reminded him of the sounds she made when his cock pushed inside her clinging channel, pleasure just a heartbeat away. He loved kissing her, deciding he'd never tire of the feel and taste of her.

When he drew back they were both breathing hard. He nuzzled the tender skin of her neck, the wet suction of his mouth making a smacking sound. Lana laughed and struggled to touch his chest, unbuttoning his shirt with urgent hands.

He slipped his hands under the hem of her dress, lifting the silky fabric so he could touch her intimately, cup the globes of her butt with his hands. Man, the woman made him ache. His dick throbbed against his fly.

"You have no idea how good this is, how much I needed sex," she said.

"Glad to be of service." Thank God he'd come to Middlemarch. He'd almost changed his mind at the last minute, thinking he needed to let more time elapse. The idea of her fucking someone else... Hell, it had been bad enough when she'd mated with Jamie. His feline stirred, agitated by his thoughts.

"Um...I hope you don't think I do this on a regular basis."

Guilt shaded her words and his alarm rose. He'd loved his cousin like a brother but he'd died. How the hell did he fight a ghost? "Of course I don't. You told me there had been no

45

one since Jamie, and besides, I noticed your tightness." Damn, they needed to change the subject. He didn't want to talk about Jamie or the past. "Turn around. Put your hands on the tree."

With his excellent night vision, he caught her shiver. His eyes narrowed, his body tensing until he heard the soft hiss of her breath. His orders turned her on. He relaxed, although took care to maintain a neutral expression.

She turned away, placing her hands on the rough tree trunk one at a time. Once settled, she glanced over her shoulder, her eyes gleaming. His ears picked up her elevated and choppy breathing. Damned sexy. Hot. His cock pulled even tighter, and he barely resisted a wince. Duncan closed the gap between them, allowing his body heat to sear her back. He pushed aside the curtain of shiny dark hair to expose her neck.

"Duncan, we need to hurry before someone comes along."

"Patience, sweetheart. Haven't you ever wondered what it would be like having someone watch you make love? How hot it would feel?"

"Embarrassing," she muttered, sounding as if she knew from experience. "I don't like giving a show."

The ghost of Jamie again. Duncan stilled, shock kicking him in the gut. *Interesting*. He wanted details except her tone didn't encourage questions. Another shift of subject required. He nuzzled the delicate skin of her neck and licked a tender spot right behind her ear. She sighed, so he did it again. Her flavor exploded across his tongue. Vanilla spice and honey. Decadent and addictive.

The sound of approaching voices made her tense and him curse under his breath. If he didn't do something quick, he'd lose her. The key to winning her was sex. He had to get her to want him, crave him. Bloody Jamie. What the heck happened in her marriage to leave these mental scars? When she stirred, he moved to both distract and reassure her. He skimmed his hands beneath her dress again, peeling silky panties down her legs.

"No one can see us here. I promise. Lift your feet for me." He held his breath while she hesitated, only releasing it when she obeyed. He bent, maneuvering the silk off her legs, over her shoes, and stuffed the panties in the rear pocket of his jeans. Then he set about seducing her.

The voices came closer and closer. Lana moaned her distress at impending discovery, but to his relief she stood firm while he petted her. He slid his hands up the inside of her thighs, knowing the friction of his rope-roughened hands against her tender skin would drive pleasure to the fore. As she pushed back her bottom, seeking a more intimate touch despite the risk of discovery, he grinned in pure relief. Man, she responded so readily, so honest in her reactions. It made him hot, his feline eager to possess and mark her. He let his fingers wander closer to her sex.

"Duncan."

At least she knew who made love to her. That was a start. He dipped his fingers into her cream, smoothing it back across her puckered rosette. "Do you want me, Lana?"

"Yes."

"What do you want me to do?"

"I want you to touch my clit," she wailed, fingers gripping the bark of the tree while pushing against him.

"I want that too," he said, dark heat flashing through him. God, did he ever. "Let me tongue you first." With light pressure on her legs, he indicated he wanted her to shift her stance. She obeyed with alacrity, her arousal a decadent scent teasing at his restraint. "That's it. Good girl. Yeah, that's perfect." Unconsciously he used the soothing tones he used while handling bulls and horses. He knelt, lifting the full skirt of her dress and kissed one thigh. Duncan heard the timbre of voices, a male and female arguing about drinking. He doubted the couple even knew they were there. With his tongue he rasped over her soft flesh, moving up to the crease of her thigh. He gripped her curvy ass with his hands, steadying her when she trembled. God, her taste and scent. The memory would be with him always—a combination of spices and sweet honey.

"Duncan, please stop teasing." Her voice held a note of strain and this time he thought it was sexual rather than anxiety at discovery in a compromising position.

Hell, it wasn't as if he could take much more of this either. His jeans tightened until he suspected a permanent zipper line etched onto his cock. His fault for discarding underwear. He raised his head and buried his face in her sweet pussy, rasping his tongue across her swollen flesh while dipping his finger into the valley running between the curves of her butt. Back and forth he licked her, tongue fluttering across her swollen nubbin, finger massaging her puckered rosette. She trembled so much he had to use one hand to steady her. Her legs tightened around his head and small cries of pleasure escaped her. Sweet. And all his—as long as he could get past her protective layers. He stroked her rosette and pushed a single finger inside while going for a direct assault on her clit. Lana gasped, a gush of juices surging against his mouth.

"Come for me, sweetheart." She trembled. "That's it, babe." He moved his finger, savoring the buck of internal muscles while he curled his tongue around and across, giving her the exact pressure she required.

Suddenly she spasmed under his tongue, her moan of pleasure humming right through him. That was what he was talking about. He'd reel her in with hot sex and pleasure. Before she knew it, he'd have his mark on her shoulder and a matching one on his. He licked her with long, luscious strokes, letting her come down slowly before he started the process over again. When she ceased shuddering, he eased away and stood. The night had become silent apart from the faint sounds of music in the distance. As he'd hoped, the owners of the voices had passed without noticing them. They were alone.

Duncan unfastened his jeans, the whine of his zipper loud enough to make Lana jump.

"Easy," he said, reverting to his soothing voice again. Two steps forward and one step back. It didn't matter. Despite his feline's urges, he could exercise patience.

He gripped his cock, his head tipping back to enjoy the pleasure of his tight, stroking hand. Hell, he hovered so close to climax it wouldn't take much more to toss him into pleasure. Fast wasn't what he wanted between them. Duncan eased behind her, moving her body with gentle hands so she leaned forward and he lifted her dress. The sight of her damp, swollen tissues filled him with pride, with lust and a sense of ownership. His woman. He guided his cock to her entrance, sliding to the hilt in one thrust.

"Damn, that feels good. Like liquid silk." Giving in to temptation, he nibbled at her neck, going close but not too close to the site at the juncture of neck and shoulder where he'd mark her soon.

"Duncan, move," she ordered, making him chuckle.

"Good things come to those who wait." *And ain't that the truth.* Heeding the soft demand in her voice, he upped the pace. He plunged into her tight channel, surging and retreating, letting the pleasure build and build. When the warning tingle of orgasm pulsed through him, he sought her clit, sliding an insistent finger over the sensitive nub. "Come for me, sweetheart. Now."

Her channel clenched his cock, and he exploded, gasping with the awe-inspiring sensations. Tight spasms milked him dry, and he stood, lungs pumping for breath, hands clutching her to his chest. Only when she stirred did he let her go and separate their bodies. In silence he dug into his pocket and pulled out a clean hanky. He handed it to her while he pushed his cock into his jeans and zipped.

"Can I sleep with you tonight?" He asked half expecting her to say no. He'd prepared for that, telling Saber earlier he'd be around later. Initially he'd thought he'd spend the night at the campsite, make sure he got plenty of sleep before his bull riding event the next day. After meeting with Lana and experiencing her skittishness firsthand, things had changed. When it came to it, he didn't care if he won the go-round or not. Lana was the prize he sought.

After a quick cleanup, Lana smoothed her dress with a swish of fabric. He accepted the hanky back and stuffed it in his pocket while waiting for his answer.

"What about Saber and Emily? What will they think?"

"I'm sure they'll understand. Besides, you've heard the gossip about the Mitchell brothers and their women. I doubt anything we do would shock them."

"I don't want to start any rumors." She stared at him for a moment before glancing down to gaze at her shoes.

"No problem," he said. Lie! A friggin' big problem when he wanted to shout their relationship from the rooftops. However, to appease Lana, he'd sneak around if that was what he had to do. "Do you want to go back to the dance or head to Saber's?"

She nibbled on her bottom lip, still refusing to look at him. "Could you take me back to the house?"

"Sure. My SUV is at the campground. It's not far to walk from here."

"Thanks."

Duncan gestured for her to precede him out of the stand of trees into the moonlight. When the path widened he took her arm, guiding her over the rough spots.

Lana walked at his side in silence. "Bother." She stopped without warning. "I left my purse with Emily. I'll have to go back and get it."

"How about if we stop there on the way out to the house? I can run in and get it for you."

She laughed, her pale face lighting up. "Won't you mind carting around a ladies purse? No telling what the other cowboys might think."

Duncan snorted. "I'm secure in my masculinity. If they want to laugh, let them. I'll get my own back when I whip their asses at the rodeo tomorrow."

They walked into a deserted campground since most of the cowboys were at the fundraiser. As promised, Duncan made a quick stop to collect Lana's bag.

"How's the restaurant going?" Duncan hated the crushing silence between them.

"Really well. We have a steady clientele along with quite a few tourists. It's hard work but I love it. Jamie said—"

To his frustration she broke off, flashed him a fake smile and sank back into silence again. "What did Jamie say? You can discuss him, you know."

"No, I can't. You were best friends and cousins. This is weird."

Weird or disloyal? Either way Duncan didn't like the way Jamie kept coming between them. "Jamie was conservative. I'll take a guess and say he'd have preferred that you didn't keep up the restaurant after you mated."

"Conservative is one word for it."

The lifting and tightening of her jaw told Duncan Jamie's traditional tendencies were a sore spot and a former source of tension between the mates. Whenever he'd seen them together they'd been happy, he thought, genuinely happy. Perhaps he'd ask around, do some subtle digging rather than talk to Lana. Emily might know something. If he explained his reasons for wanting to learn about Lana, she might even tell him. Likely tease him as well, he thought with a sigh.

Finally the silence got to him. He leaned over and started the sound system. A surreptitious glance told him the move had relaxed Lana. She'd eased into the seat and closed her eyes, listening to the lyrics of the Shania Twain ballad.

Duncan turned off the main road, driving toward the Mitchell homestead. Best he didn't mention he'd purchased land near Cromwell and not far from Queenstown. Five minutes later he pulled up outside the homestead.

"Lana, we're here." He reached over to wake her, wanting to kiss and touch her. At the last second he decided to go slow because wariness rode her like a green cowboy climbing on board an experienced rodeo bull. He grasped her shoulder, shaking her gently.

She came to life with a jolt, senses kicking in at once. "Are we home?"

Her words squeezed his heart. Hell, yeah. They were home. Lana just hadn't realized it yet.

Chapter 4

Temporary

Despite the dark interior of his SUV, he caught the faint heat in her cheeks and the widening of her eyes. It was difficult to restrain his grin.

"Maybe we shouldn't since we're in Saber and Emily's house." Lana refused to meet his gaze.

Huh, if she thought he'd back off, acting the gentleman at this late stage, she could think again. Determination tightened his hands on the steering wheel. They were back to cat and mouse again. Fine. The idea of pursuing her pumped adrenaline through him in a heated surge. They'd go through the chase for as long as it took Lana to realize they were a couple and belonged together.

"How about a coffee?"

She shot him a look of disbelief. "At this time of the night?"

"You're chucking me out? The least you can do is give me a coffee to make sure I don't run off the road on the way back to the campgrounds."

Lana made a faint huffing sound, and he had to work hard to restrain his amusement. "All right," she said. "I'd hate to have that on my conscience." She opened the door and climbed out, walking up the footpath to the front door of the homestead without waiting for him.

Duncan chuckled this time, his attention drawn to the sway of her hips as she flounced away from him. By the time he followed she was already inside. In the kitchen, he leaned against the counter and watched her, content to enjoy the way she moved as she made coffee.

"And I'd need a kiss good night," he said, breaking the silence between them.

Lana stilled, and he heard her swallow. Nerves, distaste or something else? Time to find out.

"I'll take that kiss," Duncan said, deciding to push her and his luck. Time would tell.

"Now?" Her tongue darted out to moisten her lips.

"Yeah. Do you have a problem with that?" He prowled around the edge of the kitchen counter without taking his eyes off her.

Lana dragged in a deep breath, her chest expanding with the heavy intake of air. Her pulse thudded, faster than normal while she considered his question and watched him stalk her. Yeah, stalk! The man had it down to a fine art. She wanted him to kiss her more than she wanted or needed her next breath. This thing between them, this thing that should remain casual and a mere scratching of an itch had taken on a life of its own. It had hit her during the journey back here. She'd learned something about herself. The ability to separate sex and love wasn't easy and Lana didn't think she had it in her to enjoy sex without letting her emotions become involved. Problem. A big-time problem, although on the plus side, Duncan would leave once the rodeo ended. Time would take care of the rest, and besides, she'd keep busy with the restaurant.

He reached her side and drew her into an embrace, pressing their bodies together in a nonsexual, friendly manner. Not what she'd expected. The contact seemed casual and easy despite the tension she sensed in him. Yep, she gave him a few more seconds before he lost patience and kissed her, annihilating her good intentions with a couple of smooth moves.

It was about fifteen seconds longer than she'd predicted when Duncan put space between them to study her expression, his eyes glowing with banked passion. "My kiss?"

"Oh, and I thought you'd just take it," she said with gentle mockery.

"I prefer to do things my way in the bedroom."

"How could I know that? It's not as if we've had sex in a bedroom yet."

A bark of laughter escaped him. "True, which is why I'd like to remedy the situation. Some good old-fashioned fucking in a bed followed by a little kink. What do you say?"

Lana sighed. Her body wasn't having a problem with the idea, turned on by both the idea and his frank speech. Her mind had become the problem. Too much thinking. Way too much thinking. She'd come to Middlemarch with sex on her brain. Nothing had changed after an afternoon of sex with Duncan. Nothing. She still had months and months of horniness stored up inside.

Coming to a decision, she said, "I like the idea."

"You won't change your mind again?"

"No. Do you really want coffee?"

Duncan shook his head, his gaze watchful.

"I didn't think so. Let me turn everything off and we'll hit the bedroom." Tremors shook her hands when she returned the coffee beans and mugs to the cupboard and flipped the switch on the coffeemaker. She wanted to experience his muscles flexing beneath her fingers, his cock embedded deep in her pussy surging and retreating again, needed him with surprising intensity, considering they'd had sex several times already.

"Are you dithering?"

"Dithering?" She wrinkled her nose. "What sort of word is that?" Damn, the man for being so perceptive. She was bloody procrastinating because the strength of her need scared her half to death.

"I want to know if I frighten you." He watched her, unmoving, his posture relaxed. His eyes glowed, holding heat and tension. Passion.

"You don't frighten me. I know you'd never hurt me." Not true. Lana feared he'd spoiled her for other men. Somehow the thought of having a quick weekend of sex with another man, whenever she had a gap in her schedule, didn't appeal. Damn and blast her head. Her mind was too busy. She kept thinking and had started to second-guess every decision she made. "You want to fuck me, Duncan? Let's do it."

"And what if Saber and Emily come home early? Or if one of the others arrive unexpectedly. I didn't think you enjoyed others watching you during the sexual act. You worried about someone seeing earlier."

Lana snorted. "That's not what I meant and you know it. I'm going to bed. If you want to come with me, that's fine. If not, you know where the door is." She sauntered past, giving him attitude even though inside she quivered like an inexperienced girl. But there was nothing girlish in the sexual response, the moistening of her sex and the tight sensation in her nipples. Her breath came in pants and she had to force herself to keep moving to her allocated bedroom. Lana took another two tottery steps before masculine hands spanned her waist. The next instant her world tilted, and she hung over Duncan's shoulder, looking at the passage from a new perspective.

"Put me down."

"No."

"I'll scream."

"Go ahead and scream, babe. We're going to the bedroom."

"I can go by myself. I have legs." Lana thumped her fists on his backside and his buttocks flexed as he strode along the passage.

"Which room?"

"The last one at the end. I could have walked by myself," she repeated.

"It was time for action. You were thinking too much. You'll have plenty of time to think on Monday."

Exactly what frightened her.

Inside the bedroom, he tossed her onto the bed and turned on the light.

"Strip," he said.

Lana blinked against the bright glare and stared up at him. "You want me to strip?"

"Yeah, I didn't watch you this afternoon."

"I don't want to." A lie. She wanted to obey him and that posed a problem. She'd done everything Jamie had told her to and look what happened there. As much as she'd loved Jamie and missed him, she hadn't been blind to his faults and the problems in their marriage. If Jamie had lived... Oh no! She wasn't going there. He was dead so there was no point thinking about what might have been.

Duncan's eyes narrowed, and he folded his arms across his chest. "I might as well leave then."

"You wouldn't."

"Try me."

Lana frowned. He confused the heck out of her. Combined with her own feelings, he made her head whirl. "I thought you wanted me, wanted to be with me tonight."

"I do, but I'm not willing to take half measures. It's all or nothing, Lana."

"What does it matter? We're only together for the rest of the weekend."

Duncan's frown deepened. He pushed away from the wall and crossed the carpeted floor to stare at her. "You might as well know. When it comes to sex, I like things my way. Complete compliance."

A ripple went through Lana at his words. Part of it was concern because of her experience with Jamie, but inside, interest stirred as well—a flutter of her pussy and a tightening ball of tension in the pit of her stomach. She swallowed. "I'm not sure I like the idea of being dominated. I prefer to make my own decisions."

"And I'm fine with that, except for the bedroom. I told you earlier I want to dominate the order of things."

"I see." Lana scrutinized him, searching for his intentions. Not a whisper of gossip had reached her about his sexual predilections, which meant he was both circumspect and didn't step out of line with any of his partners. She had firsthand experience of some of his techniques and had lived to tell the tale. Nothing too bad. What did she have to lose?

It was just for the weekend.

Come Sunday they'd part and mightn't see each other for six months or longer. Pushing aside her lingering worries, she shoved off the bed. Okay, if he wanted her to strip, she'd do it. Not that it would take long since she only wore a dress. A naughty frisson danced through her, bringing a rash of chill bumps to her arms and legs. Humming, she swayed, satisfaction filling her when Duncan stepped back to give her room.

His hot gaze made her wet and daring. She reached behind and slid open the zipper of her dress. Gracefully, she rolled her shoulders, letting one of the bodice straps slither down her arm to bare the upper slopes of her breasts. Continuing to sway to the tune she heard inside her head, she peeked at Duncan through lowered lashes. All male and sexy with it. He wasn't cute. No, that description didn't work for him. Masculine and confident. Lana snorted inside. Like Jamie, which should have made her scramble for cover. Instead, she'd grab the moment and tempt fate.

Duncan leaned against the wall, a smile hovering on his lips. "Is that it? Don't I get to see more skin?"

Lana breathed out with a huff of irritation. With a shrug of her shoulder the other strap slipped down her arm. She shimmied and the silky green fabric moved lower until, aided by gravity, it slithered to a pool at her feet. Lana stepped out of it and bent to pick it up. With peekaboo motions she held the fabric up to screen her naked body. Really, it seemed decadent to strut around wearing high heels and not a stitch more. At any other time she might have melted to a puddle of embarrassment, but Duncan made her nudity seem natural. Desirable.

"I'll take the dress for you." Duncan tugged it from her hands and placed it over the back of a chair so it wouldn't wrinkle. Then he let his attention wander to her, his warm eyes drifting across each one of her curves. It felt as if he were touching her physically and a shiver of pure need rippled across her skin.

"Are you going to spend the night looking at me?"

"If that's what I decide to do."

"Won't that be boring? For both of us?"

"You like me looking. Your breathing is elevated. Your breasts are swollen and ripe for my touch. And best of all, I can smell your arousal. Knowing you want me, want my touch, is very sexy. Sex is more than shoving a cock into a receptive pussy. Good sex is a state of mind. It's a banquet rather than a snack on the run. That is what I want with you tonight. A feast."

Lana's averted her gaze and fought the urge to lift her hands to cover her breasts while contrarily, her sex grew moist. A man had never seduced her with words before. The suit and tie brigade who visited her restaurant, the so-called educated businessmen didn't do this well with conversation. Their most determined flirting did nothing. This cowboy, with a few well-chosen words, had her panting for him. She swallowed and tried to regulate her choppy breathing. It didn't work. Her heart had settled into a gallop and nothing could stop the excitement pulsing through her body.

"No comment?" Duncan pushed away from the wall and prowled across the room until he reached her side. With the tip of one blunt finger he traced around a nipple. As they both watched, it drew tight and an aching sensation throbbed, working down her body. She couldn't restrain her gasp and reached for him, wanting to touch, if only to ground herself.

"No touching," he instructed. "I will do the touching for the moment."

Her breasts rose and fell with her quick inhalation. Slowly he circled her, studying her nude body. He trailed his fingers across her shoulder blade and cupped the curve of one buttock before he faced her again with the faint smile still in place.

"Beautiful. Sexy. Desirable."

With Duncan, that was exactly how she felt. "You could add impatient."

"Good things come to those who wait."

"That's what my mother used to say."

"Sounds like a wise woman."

Lana sighed. "She was. I miss her."

"No sad thoughts tonight. We're having a feast, a celebration."

"Then why am I so hungry?" Lana wailed.

Duncan chuckled. "Patience. Part your legs for me."

Obediently she shifted her stance, a little embarrassed by her arousal. Not that it seemed to bother Duncan. He pinched one nipple without warning, the surge of pain dragging free a husky protest. But the pain didn't linger, settling straight to her pussy, curling into heat and desire. Duncan leaned closer and kissed the delicate skin of her neck, giving her the faint bite of teeth and the soothing rasp of his tongue. Her breathing settled into a purr. His sinful lips moved lower, and he licked across her collarbone before the hot, tight suction of his mouth brought a jolt of dark pleasure. It speared straight to her core, the heat blossoming and plumping her folds.

"I love the way you respond."

When a man tended a woman so well with strokes and seductive licks, pleasure came easy. A mew of need escaped as his mouth neared one pouting nipple. Her pulse stalled before jumpstarting. *Now. Please take me into your mouth.* Luckily, he answered her fervent prayers, taking her nipple deep into his mouth. There was nothing gentle about it. He sucked hard, and the sensation echoed in her sex, a swift spasm of pleasure and a sensation of tightening. A purr of approval escaped.

"I like that," she murmured, her head lolling to the side.

"I know, sweetheart. Just wait. It will get better. Much better."

How could it get better? She'd experienced his lovemaking already and didn't see how he could improve. Heck, she hoped his words were all talk because if he spoke the truth, she'd be in trouble. If things got any better, she'd start to daydream about him when she should ground herself in reality and get back to her business on Monday morning.

Duncan ran callused hands over her rib cage and her hips while he shifted his mouth to her other breast. The combination of sensations flooded her mind, the drag of rough fingers over her smooth skin, the tug of his mouth at her breast, and the sounds. He murmured gentle encouragement whenever his mouth wasn't busy, praising her softness, her lush curves and her responses. Damn, she wanted to whimper. She might in a minute. All the blood in her body seemed to head south, and it pulsed in her pussy. Lana stirred, restless.

"Good girl. I'll make it better soon." He mouthed her nipple, giving her a hint of teeth.

"Hurry," she ordered.

Duncan released her nipple, letting it slip from his mouth. "We're doing things my way, remember?"

"Yeah, like the song. I can hardly forget. Your way is slow. We only have the weekend."

Not if he had anything to do with it, Duncan thought. This was only the start of something everlasting.

He moved down her body until he knelt in front of her. She shifted, redistributing her weight. The scent of her arousal wafted closer, and he screened his eyes. *Toast*. The woman wriggled past his defenses without difficulty, but he had to stay strong. Strength and determination to win her.

With pressure on her thighs, he encouraged her to spread her legs farther apart. Knowing the position could become uncomfortable soon, he upped the pace. He licked along the juncture of torso and leg, dragging his tongue downward until he neared her mons. Silky-smooth skin. God, she tempted him like no other. He rasped his tongue along her slit, parting her folds to gain access to her clit. Her honey flowed across his taste buds.

"Duncan." Lana's legs trembled, her hands grasping his shoulders for support.

Duncan rose in a smooth move, lifting her into his arms. He lowered her to the bed and followed her down to the mattress. Her beautiful eyes glowed with passion, calling to him. His cock had lengthened, and because he still wore his jeans, cramped his style. Bloody uncomfortable. Duncan adjusted himself before cupping her ass with his hands and lifting her to his mouth. With leisurely strokes of his tongue he feasted, tasting her honey and stoking her pleasure. He wanted to drive her crazy, just as she drove him wild. And if he enjoyed her meltdown, why should he argue?

She moaned, muscles tensing when he licked at her clit. Using his fingers, he filled her while he rasped his tongue down her cleft. The tiny sounds she made at the back of her throat filled him with lust and put intense pressure on his zipper, yet he wouldn't be anywhere else. He hummed and blew warm air over her nub, watching it pulse. Lana bucked under his ministrations, whispering his name.

"Soon, Lana. You can go higher yet."

"No, no, no," she chanted. "Make me come. It's so good it hurts. Please, please make me come."

His cock twitched, and he had to bite back a groan. Forcing away his desperate desire, he concentrated on Lana, the woman he wanted and had lusted after for years. The thought centered him and helped Duncan push harder. He teased and drove her higher until her limbs trembled and she lifted her hips, jerking them upward each time he licked near her clit. She pleaded and begged and shook, looking so beautiful it made his heart twist.

With the taste of her on his lips, he pulled away to survey her. Legs splayed, her sex glistening, she seemed like a wanton angel.

His.

Satisfaction coursed through his veins as he watched her, the rapid rise and fall of her chest and the restless movements of her limbs.

Lana propped up on her elbows to glare at him. "Is that it? Are you finished?" Her words rose until the final ones came out at a distinct shriek.

Suppressing a smile, he said, "Of course not. I'm going to take off my clothes, settle myself between your legs and guide my cock into place."

Her tongue darted out to moisten her lips. "And then what?"

"I'll thrust into you, pushing deep until I fill you."

Her eyes widened before she nodded. "Good idea. Hurry."

"Touch yourself while I undress," he suggested. "But not enough to make yourself come."

"While you watch?"

"You promised to obey me."

A crease furrowed her brow, and they stared at each other for a long moment—a male-and-female battle—until Lana averted her gaze. As he watched, her hand inched down her torso at a torturous pace.

Duncan bit back a curse and pushed off the bed to strip. Boots first then his clothes. He made quick work of the chore, hissing with relief when his cock sprang free. The entire time he watched Lana finger herself, sliding her digit into her pussy, coating it with her juices and bringing it back to circle her swollen clit.

"Once more," he said, kneeling on the bed beside her. While she repeated the action, he tugged one nipple, twisting it.

"You're torturing me," she complained.

"What do you want me to do?"

"I want you to shove your cock inside me for a start."

"Next time I'm bringing my bag of tricks and I'll make sure I have a gag and ropes."

Lana's mouth dropped open. He'd mentioned ropes before and she thought he'd been joking. Her teeth snapped together with an audible click. "I do not talk too much."

Duncan didn't reply. Instead he flopped onto his back and stared at her with silent expectation.

"What?"

"You wanted my cock. Take what you need."

Unbidden, her gaze swept his body to settle at his groin. His thick shaft jutted upward, the mushroom-shaped head glistening. His brows rose, and a smile curled his lips. Challenge shone in his eyes.

"A dare?"

"Yep."

Lana snorted. "I thought you were spouting about taking charge."

"And you're balking at the thought of giving control over to me. I'm making it easy for you. Take what you want." He settled with his hands under his head, watching her with clear expectancy. "Ride me."

Lana eyed his erection again and clenched her thighs together. A liquid roll of desire hit her and she had to bite back a groan. Undeniable masculine interest and the wetness pooling between her thighs spurred her to action. She clambered over his legs until she straddled him, her pulse spiking. Heck, she'd done this before so why was she so nervous?

"Carry on."

Arrogant so-and-so. Someone should teach him a control lesson. Without thinking any further, she leaned over to press a kiss to his lips, a brief skimming of mouths. Even that contact sent a bolt of lust rocketing through her, unraveling her restraint. Taking a deep breath, she settled in to kiss him. She nipped at his bottom lip, laving the sting with her tongue. Lana touched the tip of her tongue to his mouth, taking it slowly and going all out to seduce him. Increasing the pressure, she took advantage of his parted lips. She sucked his bottom lip into her mouth, licking along it with her tongue while her fingers burrowed into his dark hair. Gradually, she moved her mouth lower, kissing his jaw and trailing kisses toward his ear. He groaned when she licked the shell of his ear and nibbled his lobe, thrilled at the small sound from him. She craved his touch, but his hands remained at his sides. He truly had ceded control to her.

So she'd tempt him.

Lana licked the column of his throat and gave a little nibble at the juncture of neck and shoulder. His heartfelt curse brought surprise then a flash of panic. Fuck! What the hell was she doing? She needed to keep well away from the spot where feline shifters traditionally marked each other and made their mating official. No way did she want to give him ideas. This was a one-time deal.

Moving away from the trouble area, she rasped her tongue over one flat nipple, teasing it to attention. His fingers tangled in her hair, silent encouragement in the pressure of his hands. She knew her tongue rasped more than a human's and loved it when he licked any part of her body. His husky appreciation and the buck of his hard body brought satisfaction and pleasure.

"Kiss and lick my cock," he whispered, his breath warm against her ear.

"I have a program," she said. "There's lots of good stuff yet. I don't want to miss a thing."

"And what if I die of heart failure before you get to the extra-good stuff?"

"You? A big, bad cowboy? I thought cowboys were tough. Besides, you said I could do what I wanted."

"Nah, babe. I'm marshmallow in your hands."

"Now why don't I believe that? You want me to follow your orders, even though we're only lovers for the weekend. And you're bossy outside the bedroom arena too."

Duncan blinked once before he grinned. "I love your strong, independent spirit. It's very sexy."

"And you're avoiding the point of this conversation." Lana nipped a pectoral muscle. "You're bossy. All feline males are bossy because it's part of your nature and you don't like females who have aspirations outside the family home." Oops, she hadn't meant to lecture him. Besides, it didn't matter. After this weekend she wouldn't see him again for months.

Lana leaned over to lick his ribs and his splendid abs, allowing her hair to fall forward and curtain her chagrin. Bother Jamie and his old-fashioned rules about women. Babies. She wasn't unnatural because she didn't want children straightaway. One day she'd love to have children, and meanwhile, being on the Pill protected her from an unwanted pregnancy. Huh, that and abstaining from sex. She dipped her tongue into his navel before licking around the indentation, smiling at Duncan's purr of pleasure. Just as she suspected. Males liked a little petting before getting to the main course.

She moved lower still, letting her fingers trail over his abs and work-hardened muscles. Lana knew he worked on farms and ranches between rodeos. His soapy and masculine scent curled through her while his rough purrs brought a deepening smile.

Instead of heading straight for his jutting cock, she kissed his inner thighs, breathing in his scent and dragging it deep into her lungs. Her hands skimmed with purpose and skill, driving both their arousals higher.

Duncan sighed, his hips canting upward when she nuzzled his balls. She'd half expected him to take over again, but instead, he watched her through heavy-lidded eyes, his thighs spreading to give her better access. The velvety head of his cock brushed her cheek and Lana swallowed, excited by his trust and her rising desire. She dragged her tongue along his length, kissing the curving glans at his tip.

"Lana," he whispered.

He packed a lot of meaning into the one word, a lot of need. A hungry little noise emerged from deep in her throat and she licked the length of his cock again before repeating the kiss. This time she sealed her lips around the head and sucked. His entire body jolted, driving him deeper into her mouth. The musky taste and his scent him filled each of her breaths.

"Take more," he said.

She wanted to please him and obeyed, even before she realized he'd wrested control from her. Didn't matter. All that mattered was the pleasure that rippled between them, the passion that sprang to life when they touched. Lana took him deep and swirled her tongue over the head while she scraped her fingers over his balls. They drew tighter with her ministrations and tension swirled between them. Her sex throbbed, and as if he could read her mind, Duncan seized her by the shoulders, lifting her head from his cock.

"Take me inside you. Ride me. I want your snug pussy gripping my cock. I want to watch your beautiful breasts bounce while you take me. And I want to see you rubbing your clit. I want you to take your pleasure. I want to watch your face when you come."

"What about you?"

"I'm a big boy. I can take care of myself."

Lana didn't doubt that for a moment. Trembling, she lifted her body and guided his cock to her entrance. She impaled herself, closing her eyes to savor the stretch as his cock parted her sensitive tissues. The brush of fingers over the curves of her breasts made her smile dreamily, but the caress of her marking spot had her eyes flying open. They stared at each other, silent messages gliding back and forth between them. Lana swallowed.

Too much. Too intimate.

She rose off his cock and sank down again, keeping each move slow and purposeful while her mind screamed at her to do something, to flee the temptation that had seized her by the throat. Another swallow shifted the lump of apprehension. Duncan was temporary. She could not, would not mate with him.

Chapter 5

Rodeo!

Something shifted between them when he touched her shoulder. A new awareness pulsed in her expression and Duncan fought past his urge to act caveman. He trailed his fingers across the smooth golden skin again, her shiver bringing a sense of satisfaction. Jamie would have marked her although it had faded. It was only a matter of time before she bore his mark. He could wait. He *would* wait until Lana accepted him readily.

Lana rode him with a steady rise and fall, pausing each time he was fully seated to squeeze her inner muscles. Hot, easy glides followed by a viselike squeeze set the pattern. His balls tightened and drew up, his cock lengthened and started to throb. She licked her lips, an unhurried and sexy moistening of the plump, pink curve.

"Touch yourself," he said when he didn't think he could hold back his orgasm for much longer.

Her chin shot up in defiance until the beginnings of a grin twitched at his lips.

"Do it," he ordered.

Her cheeks flushed as she slid her hand over her stomach. One finger slipped between her folds and she massaged her clit.

"Good girl. Show me your finger. Show me how wet you are."

"You can see I am," she retorted.

"I want to taste you."

Her eyes widened, but she dipped her finger into her juices and removed it, leaning forward so he could take the digit into his mouth.

Duncan heard her gasp and felt the subtle clamp of her pussy around his width. He sucked on her finger and watched her eyes widen. When he licked the pad before releasing it, she moaned.

"Hot and spicy. Beautiful." He leaned forward to tongue her breasts, giving her a hint of teeth and glorying in her open pleasure. It was clear she enjoyed sex as much as him, which boded well for the future.

After one final lick, Duncan settled back on the bed, encouraging her with a grin. "Make me come."

Instantly the tension ramped upward. She hastened her pace, her head falling back as she swayed above him. Sounds of fucking filled the air along with soft sighs and moans. Faster and faster she went, her tight channel squeezing him. Her finger slid across her clit while she pinched one of her nipples with her other hand. She came in a rapid explosion, her pussy pulsing around his dick. Duncan loved the play of emotions on her face, the rush of pleasure and dazed expression.

With an explosion of power, he moved, turning their bodies and fucking her hard and fast with rapid thrusts of his cock. Orgasm hit him like a rodeo bull intent on revenge. He groaned at the rush of pleasure while his semen splashed deep inside her. For an instant he stilled, his pulse fast and choppy. Hell, sex had never been this good. Closing his eyes, he rolled so Lana curled against his chest. Neither of them spoke, and that didn't matter. Duncan relaxed, comfortable and at home for the first time in his life and knew the woman in his arms played a large part in the situation. This was right, and he looked forward to a future with Lana.

Lana played the coward and pretended to be asleep when Duncan left the next morning. She knew he'd need to get back to the campground and check his equipment. When the front door closed and his steps had receded, Lana opened her eyes and turned over to flop onto her back. Her body ached in a good way and although tired, vigor danced through her veins. A little sex and hey, presto, energy zapped through her. She felt good, really good. A smile curved her lips. Who needed pills and tonics when a man like Duncan Ross was there for the taking?

A light knock jolted her upright. She clutched the sheet to her naked breasts and frowned at the door.

"Lana? Are you awake?" Emily asked.

"If she wasn't before, she is now," Saber murmured.

Lana heard feminine amusement before she replied. "I'm awake."

"Good, come and have coffee with me. I'm starved for feminine conversation."

"You talked to her yesterday and last night," Lana heard Saber say.

"I'll have a quick shower to wake up and be there in ten minutes," Lana said, climbing from the bed.

"A woman on time," Saber said when she walked into the kitchen and dropped into a chair beside Emily.

"I'm used to quick showers."

"Did Duncan get away all right?" Emily asked, shunting a mug of coffee in Lana's direction. "Do you need milk?"

"Um, no," Lana said, unsure of where to look. Finally she gave up and grinned back at Emily. If she'd thought Duncan wouldn't get the wrong idea, she might have asked if they could meet up every six months, but she didn't want to encourage him into thinking they might have something permanent. No, this way was better. She got to have fulfilling sex with a hunky male and kept her independence. Once she returned to Queenstown, she'd be flat out with the renovations to her restaurant and planning the new season's menu.

Emily's eyes twinkled over the top of her coffee mug. "Did you and Duncan have a fight?"

"Sweetheart, leave the poor woman alone. We know Duncan was here last night," Saber said. "And I doubt there was much fighting."

"Pooh, you're no fun," Emily said. "What time are we going to the rodeo? Do we want to watch the kiddies and novice events?"

"If we go early, we'll find a good place to watch the action," Lana said.

"I agree. I'll load the umbrella and the chairs into my vehicle as soon as we eat," Saber said.

Two hours later Saber left her and Emily settled in a shady spot with a good view of the rodeo arena. Country music blared through loudspeakers, a song where the male singer tried to cajole his ladylove into marriage. Lana could see a bright red-and-yellow bouncy castle on the other side of the arena and heard the shrieks of excited children. A mini Ferris wheel spun lazily while a bouquet of hot dogs, chips and meat pies filled the air.

Cattle in pens mooed and horses neighed. Cowboys sauntered past dressed in faded jeans and chaps, hats pulled low over their faces while they entered events, paid their fees at the office and concentrated on the job to come.

Emily handed Lana a glass of sparkling wine and orange juice before returning the wine and juice bottle to the chiller box. "It's a pity Saber's brothers are away this weekend. The single ones. I could have set you up with one of the twins, or not, since you're with Duncan."

Lana groaned. "No matchmaking, Emily. I have no intention of marrying again. I enjoy my independence. Besides, the twins are too young for me." She spotted London Allbright and Gerard Drummond on the other side of the arena and waved when they looked in her direction.

"Really? Hmm, you could be right about Joe and Sly. We don't see them often." She cocked her head, reminding Lana of a curious bird. "Don't you want a man to keep you warm during the cold winter nights? And children?"

"I don't need to be married to do either of those," Lana pointed out.

"Don't take this the wrong way, but there are so few feline women of marriageable age. What about the pressure to mate?"

"First off, I loved Jamie. Things changed because we clashed about children. During the last three months of our marriage, we'd started to argue. Jamie wanted to start a family. I wanted to keep growing my business. Before we married I told him my plans and he agreed to wait to have children. Jamie had grown tired of waiting and was pressuring me. We argued before he left to go skiing." A wave of memories hit her—the bitter words between them and the pain at knowing the last time they'd seen each other had been on bad terms. Recalling their last argument always brought guilt.

"Oh Lana. I'm sorry. That can't have been easy. Not all men are the same though."

Lana shrugged. "I'm not marrying again. It's better that way."

Emily smiled even though her eyes remained somber. "Maybe I should send Saber's twin brothers to your restaurant. I swear you won't be able to resist either of them."

"I met them at the wedding, remember. Yes, they're both nice and very sexy. I'm not interested."

"They're bad boys through and through, you mean."

"I was being polite," Lana said. "They would need a lot of training."

"Their future wives are lucky. I've started training them already," Emily said with a smirk. "Or at least I do when they deign to come home."

Both women laughed before an announcement on the loudspeaker drew their attention to the arena.

The morning passed quickly with the children's sheep ride, the skillful barrel racers and the novice bull riders. Saber returned along with several friends and neighbors. Lana looked for Duncan and saw him at a distance talking to two scantily clad women in shorts and bikini tops. One even had the effrontery to kiss him on the lips.

"Lana? Something wrong?"

Lana jerked her gaze away to stare at Saber. "Huh?"

"You were growling," Emily said.

"Oh! I was thinking about work and one of the companies I deal with," she said, hoping her pitiful save would work. This jealousy had to stop. First, she had no right. And second, Duncan came in the temporary entertainment category and didn't owe her anything. She accepted a chicken salad wrap

81

from Emily and a glass of straight orange juice from Saber before she risked another glance. He wasn't in sight now and the two women were chatting up another cowboy. Funny, when they both kissed this man she didn't experience the zing of jealousy.

"When is the open bull ride starting?" she asked.

"Duncan's event?" Emily glanced at the program. "One o'clock."

One of Saber's friends settled beside Lana and started chatting. The glint in his eyes told Lana of his interest. He seemed nice enough except her thoughts drifted to Duncan. Instant attraction. It had been the same with Jamie. She'd taken one look and wanted him.

These days she had grown smarter and knew all the love in the world didn't make a successful relationship. Marriage was hard work and an added stress came for shifters—the pressure to have children. Not that she didn't like kids, because she did. It was just there were other important things in life such as personal fulfillment.

Echoes of Jamie's last words, calling her a selfish bitch, propelled another wave of guilt through her. Perhaps she was selfish. All the more reason to stay single and concentrate on the business she loved.

The parade of nations opened the afternoon's events with horses galloping around the arena, their riders bearing flags of the countries who promoted rodeo.

A brief lull followed before a voice over the loudspeaker system announced the start of the open bull ride.

"First out of the chute today is William Edwards on Demon Express," the announcer said.

A brindle bull exploded from the chutes with a loud bellow of displeasure, lethal horns catching Lana's attention. Demon Express tossed his rider with one vicious corkscrew buck, sending the cowboy hurtling through the air. He hit the dusty ground, and the bull charged over him, catching the man with a glancing blow in the middle of his back. One of the two rodeo clowns sprinted over and drew the bull's attention while the second helped the stunned cowboy to his feet and to safety.

"A quick ride," the announcer said as the pick-up riders herded Demon Express from the arena.

Lana stared at the chutes, terror and anxiety overtaking her without warning. She'd attended rodeos before and had even known some of the cowboys. Sometimes they fell, although injuries hadn't bothered her too much. The thought of watching Duncan take a spill sickened her. Confused, she tore her attention from the arena and attempted to chat to the man seated on her right. Like her, he was a shifter, a farmer who lived near the Mitchells. He seemed nice enough, although he wasn't Duncan.

Only natural. She'd spent the last day with Duncan and they'd slept together. That was the reason for her loyalty. Nothing else.

"They say bull riding is the most dangerous eight seconds in professional sports," Rick said.

Not what she wanted to hear.

"Don't worry," Emily said. "Duncan knows what he's doing."

"Duncan?" Rick asked. "Are you with Duncan?"

"No," Lana said.

"Yes," Emily said at the same time.

Saber chuckled. "One of them is right, Rick."

Lana caught Rick's disappointment even though he hid it. "I was going to ask you to dance tonight."

"And I'll say yes," Lana said.

"She'll also be dancing with Duncan during the night," Emily said, muddying the waters again. "She's a free spirit."

Lana glared at Emily without dampening her friend's unrepentant smile. A quick glance at Rick didn't help with Lana's irritation. The speculative look in his eyes had nothing to do with finding a mate. He was thinking booty call all the way. Huh! She might want sex but she wasn't easy.

Duncan waited for his ride with the other cowboys. Normally the nerves kicked in by now. Not today. Since he'd decided to retire at the end of the season, he'd relaxed and enjoyed himself, shooting the breeze with the other cowboys and friends made on the circuit. Instead of thinking about his upcoming ride on Major, the bull he'd drawn, his thoughts drifted to Lana. The more time he spent with her the more convinced he became of the rightness of them as a couple. Jamie, his cousin, stood between them like a silent sentinel. His hand flexed around the railing of the yards where the bulls waited. There was something in Jamie and Lana's relationship that appeared off. Every time someone mentioned Jamie, Lana's reaction seemed tinged with guilt. Had she cheated on Jamie? That could be a possibility. Knowing both Jamie and Lana, it didn't seem likely. But what other reason could Lana have for remorse?

Whitie, the cowboy in front of him in the draw, climbed into the chute, one of his spurs rattling as it knocked against his other boot.

"Duncan, you're good to go in chute two," one of the behind-scenes helpers said.

Duncan pulled on his protective vest, shunting thoughts of Lana to the back of his mind before striding over to the chute. Major was a top bull. He'd need his wits about him to last eight seconds on the champion. Major's fabulous corkscrew bucks were famous. If a cowboy lasted the distance on him, they placed, often in first. Duncan had drawn Major once before and to his chagrin hadn't lasted past the second explosive buck out of the chute.

The hooter sounded, and the crowd cheered. "That was Whitie Bolton on Sinbad, the only cowboy so far to last eight seconds."

Duncan tugged a glove from his jeans pocket and drew it on his right hand. He checked the rosin, the sticky substance applied to give extra grip, and applied a little more. Emptying his mind of everything apart from Lana, he climbed up onto the chute rails to study Major, the massive crossbred Brahma bull he'd drawn. Top of the bull standings, only a handful of cowboys had ridden him to eight seconds.

Major snorted as the helpers fastened the flank strap and bull rope around his bulk. He stood quietly. Duncan didn't relax since he'd seen this before.

"Hey, boy," he murmured. "Let's you and I come to an agreement."

One stockman snorted. "This is new. Dunc is trying to talk him into submission."

The other stockman hooted. "Seems to work with the ladies. You going to the dance tonight?"

"Sure," Duncan said, taking their teasing in his stride. While they poked fun at each other, the crowd following the rodeo was a tight-knit bunch. He'd miss them when he left the circuit. His involvement as a stock contractor would be different. He'd still need to travel, but if things went the way he wanted, he'd have Lana at his side. "I'm not knocking back a chance to dance with the ladies."

"Make sure you leave some for us, mate," one said.

"I'm not greedy," Duncan said. All he wanted was one green-eyed lass called Lana. The rest he'd leave for the other men.

As Duncan climbed onto the quivering bulk of the bull, Major snorted and tossed his head. Duncan ignored him, knowing his feline scent stirred the animal's unease. Nothing like a little extra challenge to give a cowboy determination. He'd worked with the handicap from his first ride on a bull, and while some might see it as a disadvantage, Duncan thought it made him a better athlete.

"Whoa, steady there, Major," one of the stockmen said. "Haven't seen him act like this. He's usually as docile as a lamb until he springs from the chute."

"Must be me," Duncan said with unconcern, having experienced it before. He settled himself on the broad back, planted his hat on his head and adjusted his grip on the bull rope. When the all clear sounded, Duncan clamped his legs around the bull's middle, nodded his head and the gate opened.

"This is Duncan Ross riding the champion bull Major. Only a handful of cowboys have ridden this bull for eight seconds," the announcer shouted, his voice rising in excitement.

Major exploded from the chute, springing high and tucking his bulky body into his signature corkscrew. The bull landed hard, jarring Duncan's entire torso before spinning and kicking back in a series of spine-jarring twists. Dust rose in a cloud, obscuring his vision. Duncan's hat went flying. The crowd roared, but he focused on the quivering mass of muscle beneath him and on his technique. He kept his left hand high and well away from both himself and the bull to prevent disqualification. He remained loose, letting his body flow with the bull's bucks.

Nothing fancy required because Major was an athlete too. *Hang on. Stay aboard.* Another buck snapped his body upright. The wind whistled past his ears. Duncan slipped. One more tricky twist from the bull and he'd be history. He rode out a smaller, less powerful buck, regaining his balance.

Hot damn, the hooter must be close. *Stay on*. He could do it, go out as a winner. Fuck, this was a long eight seconds. Major spun and Duncan lurched to the side.

The hooter blared.

The crowd roared. He worked to free his hand and flew off, landing with a breath-stealing thump. Sometimes it was damn harder to get off a bull than clambering on. Behind him, the thunder of the pick-up horses galloped in his direction. Major bellowed and bucked off his trailing rope. The horses caught up, the riders herding the bull away, leaving Duncan to catch his breath.

"Great ride for Duncan Ross. Eight seconds on Major. That's one for the history books," the announcer screamed.

Duncan clambered to his feet and sauntered back to grab his hat, slapping it against his chaps before planting it on his head again. Grinning, he waved to the crowd, adrenaline still pumping. As he climbed the railings to exit the arena, he scanned the crowd hoping to see Lana. Disappointment hit him in the gut when he couldn't see her. He jumped off and the other cowboys mobbed him with congratulations on his ride.

"Good one, Dunc," Whitie said. "You've got a good chance at the championship this year."

"Don't think so," Duncan said. "I'm retiring."

The questions flew quick and fast, many of his friends telling him he was bloody mad. Too bad. Making his move on Lana had helped him decide. Time to retire and start a new life. If he played his cards right, Lana and he might have a kid on the way soon. He imagined Lana, her belly swollen with their child, and smiled. What a beautiful sight that would be, and if he had his way, they'd have children soon.

A cold chill rippled across Lana's skin when she watched the massive bull burst from the chutes with Duncan on its back. It struck her then how dangerous the sport was. A man could die or end up injured from taking part. She swallowed, not wanting to watch yet unable to tear her gaze away. *Please don't fall*. Her lips moved in a silent prayer as the longest eight seconds of her life played out. The hooter went and the people around her sprang to their feet, cheering and whistling. Lana remained seated because she didn't think her legs would hold her.

In that moment, her feelings crystallized with distinct clarity. She'd fallen for Duncan. Oh, she wasn't stupid enough to let him get closer, but she'd allowed her emotions to become involved. A dangerous situation and one she needed to quash before things roared out of control.

Sex was one thing. Marriage was out of the question.

Lana wasn't afraid to make mistakes. Slip-ups happened. The crime occurred when a person didn't pay attention and learn the first time 'round.

Chapter 6

Still Temporary

Lana thought about telling Duncan she couldn't sleep with him again after the rodeo dance and presentation. She'd decided it would be best to avoid both him and temptation. But one glance across the crowded room and she knew she'd been fooling herself.

Revelers packed the marquee. A Country Western band belted out foot-stompin' tunes and dancers filled the open ground serving as a dance floor. Lana sat with Emily, waiting for Saber to return with drinks. Duncan stood with a group of his friends near the entrance to the marquee. Although he appeared to listen to the conversation, his gaze swept the room. Looking for her? Her heart pounded at the thought, which made her frown. A relationship with Duncan threatened her freedom, everything she wanted for her future.

"Would you like to dance?" Rick, Saber's neighbor, tapped her on the shoulder and smiled at her. "Hi, Emily. Is it okay if we leave you alone?"

"Go and dance. Saber will be back soon. He's at the bar," Emily said.

"I'd love to." Lana pushed back her chair and stood, accepting his outstretched hand. Maybe dancing with other men would take her mind off Duncan.

Or not.

She sensed the second Duncan spotted her, the visual caress when he scanned her form. Without conceit, Lana knew she looked her best. She'd gone to extra pains, borrowing a red dress from Emily. Her lucky dress, Emily had said, pressing it into her hands even though she'd protested the dress she'd packed was fine.

A slow dance started and Rick took her into his arms, heat from his touch seeping through the silky red fabric of her dress. He smelled good, danced well and seemed a nice guy—except he wasn't Duncan. Oh boy. She was screwed.

Panic unfurled in the pit of her stomach while she gave herself a pep talk. Definitely no sex after the dance.

"Would you go out with me some time?" Rick asked.

"I don't get much time off, but I'd love to see you next time you're in Queenstown."

Rick guided her around another couple. "Is there someone else?"

"No, my restaurant keeps me busy. I'm only here this weekend because the restaurant is closed for renovations."

Rick turned her again and her gaze met Duncan's. The heat in his green eyes made her stumble. Oh yeah. She was in big, big trouble.

"Dance with me, Duncan," a feminine voice said.

Duncan dragged his attention off Lana and turned. "Hey, Jennifer. You look good tonight."

The blonde glowed with pleasure. "Thanks. Congratulations on winning the bull ride today. You were fantastic."

"Thanks. We'll dance later, hmmm? There's someone I need to see." When the music wound to an end, Duncan strode over to Lana without looking back. "Lana. Rick."

"Great ride today, Duncan," Rick said.

"Thanks. Can I steal Lana for a dance?"

Rick looked as if he might argue. Duncan didn't let that bother him. He took Lana's hand and tugged her into his arms. The notes of a slow dance started, which gave him an excuse to hold her close.

"You look beautiful."

"You scrub up pretty good yourself," Lana said.

"Is something wrong?" He registered her unease, her fear.

"Just thinking about work. I have a lot to do next week before the restaurant reopens."

"Can I help with anything?"

"Not really. Besides, you'll be off to the next rodeo."

Duncan wanted to tell her he'd retired, but she seemed so skittish he decided to wait. Some of the gossip might reach her tonight. If he stayed at her side, he'd deflect the worst. Of course he could always persuade her to take a walk and go home early.

He drew her closer to prevent a collision and her breasts brushed his white shirt.

"What are you wearing under that dress?" he asked when he noticed her rigid nipples.

She swallowed and refused to look at him. "I borrowed the dress from Emily and my bra didn't work with the cut of the bodice." An attractive flush filled her cheeks.

Duncan grinned and leaned closer to whisper in her ear. "You are wearing panties, right?"

"No," Lana said. "Emily said the dress sat better without underwear."

"Did she? I will have to thank Emily for her thoughtfulness." His hand smoothed over her back to rest on the curve of her buttocks. "Feel what you do to me."

"It's a good idea the lights are dimmed in this part of the marquee. You wouldn't want to shock any of the elderly ladies or the Feline council."

"We could take a walk," he suggested.

"Oh no. You're not talking me into that again. Besides, you need to stick around for the prize-giving."

Unfortunately she was right. "Later after the prize-giving."

SHELLEY MUNRO

"I don't think so," Lana said.

Duncan's eyes narrowed. She meant more than the prize-giving. "I'll see you later at Saber's house."

"No, not tonight."

"Why not? I thought you enjoyed last night."

"I did," Lana said. "Our night was a one-time thing. I'm heading home tomorrow and we won't see each other for months. I thought you realized I wanted sex without promises."

"You wanted to scratch an itch?"

Lana nodded. "Exactly. I told you that straight up. Whew, for a minute there I thought you'd misunderstood me. I'm not looking for serious."

Duncan nodded. *Not if he had anything to do with it.* Thanking the instinct that had told him to stay quiet regarding his retirement, he pondered his options and kept coming back to the same one. He'd have to woo her to his way of thinking.

"Lana, I know you don't want serious. That's no reason to deprive both of us of a night of fun."

"I don't know—"

"Come on, babe. It's one night and the next day we'll go our separate ways." But not for long. He was tired of the cat-and-mouse game.

"I...I'll think about it."

A challenge. A goal to work toward. He responded well to challenges. "I'll be my persuasive best," he promised.

"You don't own me," she snapped, her tone sharp and eyes flashing with sudden temper.

94

"Of course I don't." Surprised, he studied her tight-lipped expression. What the hell had gone on between her and Jamie? He'd seen them together when he came home for visits. They'd seemed happy enough. Not that he'd cared to look too closely with his emotions involved. No, instead he'd played hard, trying to forget the one woman he couldn't have. "I'd like to spend tonight with you." Pulling her close again, he guided them around the floor, just enjoying having her in his arms.

The song finished and someone tapped him on the shoulder. "Can I dance with Lana?" Rick asked.

Lana smiled. Duncan's hands tightened on her shoulders before giving the man a curt nod and stepping back. He forced himself to walk away and struggled to contain the possessive reaction flooding his body. Even so, a feral growl escaped, luckily covered by the start of the next song. He stalked across the floor, hands fisted at his side, his gums aching as canines pushed to the surface. Damn, he had to control his feline. Part of him wanted to leave while the other part wanted to return to the dance floor and tear Lana from Rick's arms. He did neither. Instead, he strode over to the table where Emily and Saber sat and claimed one of the empty chairs.

Aware of their silent scrutiny, Duncan dragged in a deep breath, clutching at the tabletop while trying to regain control. When he glanced down, he noticed his claws were visible beneath his fingernails and stuffed them out of sight. Hot damn. He hadn't had problems with control since the age of thirteen, during his randy teenager stage. His attention wandered to the dance floor, and he glimpsed Lana. Her partner's hand strayed downward until it covered her butt. A snarl squeezed past his clenched teeth and his knuckles turned white.

"Problem?" Saber asked.

Duncan blinked and realized Saber and Emily scrutinized him, aware of his turmoil. "No problem," he said before changing his mind. "Lana."

"Oh," Emily said with a grin. "Good choice."

"All she wants is a fling." Duncan tried to hide his discouragement. He'd hate for them to think less of Lana because she wanted casual sex.

Emily's grin widened to delight. "And you want more."

"You're a doomed man if you're at that stage," Saber said. "Nothing to do except follow through."

"He's already followed through," Emily said. "You heard them from our bedroom. It's stickability that's the problem."

"Not on my end," Duncan said. "Do either of you know much about her marriage to Jamie?"

"From what I could see they were happy," Saber said. "We didn't see them often in Middlemarch."

"I didn't know Jamie. He died before I met Saber. Lana hasn't discussed her marriage. We talk about girl stuff and our businesses."

"Aren't men a girl topic?" Duncan asked.

Emily picked up her glass of wine to take a sip. "You might come into the conversation."

"So you haven't heard anything?" Duncan thought she sounded evasive. Perhaps Lana had told her something in confidence. He wouldn't ask, but it gave credence to his theory. Jamie and Lana hadn't had the perfect marriage.

"No. Have you checked with Jamie's friends?" Saber asked.

Duncan shrugged. "I don't want rumors to get back to Lana."

"How can you have a relationship with Lana anyway?" Emily asked. "You're following the rodeo circuit and she has her restaurant." Her eyes narrowed. "Surely you don't expect her to give up her business?"

"It's not public knowledge yet. I'm retiring from rodeos. I'm sick of the constant moving and I miss being with other felines."

Saber nodded, understanding in his eyes. "What are you going to do?"

"I've purchased land not far from Cromwell. I hope to breed cattle suitable for the rodeo circuit and go into the stock contracting business, start a school where I can teach novice cowboys who want to go into bull riding."

"Does Lana know?" Emily asked.

"I wanted to tell her. She seemed skittish, so I decided not to say anything."

Emily frowned. "She won't react well if she learns you've known for a while and didn't tell her."

"No matter which way I approach the problem she will be pissed," Duncan said.

"I'd suggest you dance with the other girls. Don't make it look as if you're stalking her," Emily said. "Besides, a little of competition might do her good."

"Make her jealous, you mean?"

"No, I wouldn't go that far. Just make it seem as if you want a casual relationship and she might relax more," Emily said.

"Saber, you have a devious wife."

Saber took Emily's hand in his and winked at her. "She'll come in handy finding mates for the twins. I've had little success on my own."

"Where are your brothers? I thought they'd be here for the rodeo," Duncan said. "I was looking forward to meeting Leo's and Felix's wives."

"The twins are in Dunedin and Leo dragged Felix up to Wellington. They had tickets for the Sevens rugby tournament. Tomasine and Isabella decided they'd tag along and do some shopping."

"I guess I'll catch up with them over the next few months," Duncan said. The music ended and Duncan saw Lana was dancing with another man. It looked like Samuel, one of Saber's friends. "I might as well take Emily's advice and ask someone else to dance."

Duncan wandered off, leaving Saber and Emily alone.

"I thought the mating heat kicks in if a couple is compatible," Emily said in an undertone.

"Generally, a man can sense his mate and is compelled to claim her. I didn't sense undercurrents between them, although Duncan is having trouble controlling his feline. That's a sign something is up."

"Duncan has traveled a lot and learned to suppress his feline. Maybe his control is so good that the normal signs aren't present yet," Emily suggested.

"I'm just glad it's not me." Saber scooted his chair closer to Emily's. "Would you like to dance, Mrs. Mitchell?"

"I'd love to, Mr. Mitchell."

"What do you think about a walk afterward?" His eyes gleamed with both heat and mischief.

"We could, Mr. Mitchell. I will take custody of my panties," she said as a distinct afterthought.

Saber chuckled. "Maybe," he said. "Or maybe not."

Lana watched Duncan walk over to a group of women with conflicted feelings.

"Lana?"

"Oh sorry? I didn't catch that," she said to Saber's friend. Dang, she had to stop thinking about Duncan.

"I wondered if you want to go for a walk."

Heck, what was with the males tonight? They all wanted to get her outside and alone. They all had one-track minds.

"Thanks, normally I'd like that. I'm meeting with friends," she lied. "I'd hate to miss them."

"One more dance?" he asked.

"Sure." He tugged her closer, and she decided it would be better to strike up a conversation rather than letting him smooch. She didn't want to give him the wrong idea. "What sort of stock do you raise on your farm?"

He started to talk, and she relaxed, finding him a good conversationalist. The topic drifted from farming to friends in common. Lana answered easily, able to concentrate on the other dancers and her partner. A familiar face made her stiffen—Duncan on the floor, dancing with another woman. The blonde clung to him. Lana bit on her inner lip, aghast at the surge of jealousy blindsiding her. Basically, she'd told Duncan to go away, so why should it matter if he was with another woman?

The bracket of songs ended and her partner escorted her back to the table. Emily and Saber had disappeared, but Duncan arrived not long afterward. He took a swig from his bottle of beer.

"Do you mind if I leave you alone?" he asked after her partner disappeared to buy drinks. "I see a friend over there and wanted to ask her to dance."

"I don't mind," Lana said, forcing a smile. She was not jealous. *She was not*.

"Great." Duncan strolled off without looking back, and Lana stared after him in shock. Heck, what was she thinking? She had no claim on Duncan. The shifter had followed the rules she'd set for him, so how could she complain?

Another of Saber's neighbors asked her to dance, and she accepted because of politeness. That was what she told herself. In truth, she wanted to watch Duncan in action. She slipped into the man's arms and wished the band would play the faster numbers again. Duncan and his partner were dancing way too close. Her hands curled into her partner's shoulders as she watched the woman reach up to press a quick kiss to Duncan's mouth. A growling rumble rippled through her before she could control the sound.

"Are you okay?" Her partner gave her a strange look and didn't hold her quite as tight.

Lana blinked. "I'm fine."

"Are you sure? Your fingernails are digging into my shoulders."

"Oh, I'm so sorry!" Mortified, Lana curled her fingers into her palms and continued dancing. She winced at the sharp claws that had bled through from beneath her fingernails and instead smiled, moving gracefully with her partner. The lapse helped her come to a decision.

Her and Duncan.

Tonight.

When he asked again, she'd say yes. And if he thought her indecisive, too bad. It was a woman's prerogative.

Another hour passed and Lana lost count of the number of men she danced with. In between she chatted with Emily and Saber and reacquainted herself with the Middlemarch locals.

"Have you thought any more about tonight?" a voice whispered in her ear.

Duncan. She could tell by his scent, although the floral perfume didn't please her. "Yes," she said in a flat tone.

"Great. You don't sound pleased with your decision," Duncan said, taking a seat beside her.

"I'm tired." And jealous.

"You'll have to make sure you get plenty of sleep."

Lana chuckled, attracting attention. "How am I going to do that?"

"Private joke?" Emily asked.

"Lana said she's too tired to dance with me," Duncan said.

"I'll dance with you, Duncan."

Lana turned to glimpse a beautiful blonde woman. She looked familiar although Lana didn't know her name.

"All right, Jennifer. Lana, Emily, this is Jennifer. She's a barrel racer."

"I thought you looked familiar," Lana said. "You won the barrel race event today. Congratulations."

"Thanks. Come on, Duncan. This is one of my favorite songs." Jennifer took Duncan's hand and dragged him toward the dance floor.

"Lana, you're growling," Emily whispered.

"Damn. I don't feel well," Lana said. "I might see if Duncan will take me back to your place after this dance."

Emily nodded, her eyes twinkling. "That might be a good idea, but don't forget the prize-giving."

"Bother. I'll try to hold on until then."

Emily checked her watch. "They're starting in another five minutes."

"I don't understand why they didn't have it earlier," Lana muttered.

"They wanted to make plenty of money on the ticket sales and bar."

"How silly of me."

The band finished their segment and took a break. In the break, the president of the Middlemarch Rodeo Club strode to the mike on the small dais while a svelte redhead, who Lana didn't recognize, sashayed over to the prize table, set up to the right of the bar.

The prize-giving seemed endless. Lana tapped her foot, clapping dutifully for each recipient even though her head throbbed. Duncan beamed when he received his check and plaque for first place in the bull ride.

"Way to go, Duncan!" a woman he'd danced with shouted.

When the ribald comments started, females comparing bull riding and sex, Lana started growling.

"Lana," Emily said, following up her warning with a kick under the table.

"Ow!" She glared at Emily, and when she glanced at Rick, she noticed he was looking at her strangely. Cripes, she'd never had this problem before, always being in total control of her feline. Aghast, she reached for her drink and took a swig of wine. Tonight couldn't finish soon enough. Tomorrow she'd return to her own turf and her life would be in balance again—just the way she liked it.

When the presentation ended, she grabbed her bag and stood. "My head is pounding so I'm heading home. See you in the morning."

"Wait, Saber will take you," Emily said.

"No, don't worry. Duncan said he'd take me back. I'll find him." She wandered to the exit, searching for Duncan, giving her feline senses full rein to locate him. Her feline might as well be of some use today. She found Duncan standing outside with a group of his rodeo friends. Several were smoking, wisps of white spiraling into the air when they exhaled.

Lana strode over to them and came to an abrupt halt when her heels sank into the grass. "Hell and damnation." She yanked her shoes from the dirt, hot anger taking a tighter grip on her. Her eyes stung and for an awful moment she thought she might cry. Aghast, she swallowed and thought of her restaurant.

What on earth was wrong with her? With everything right in her world and her restaurant coming along nicely, she should be happy and full of beans. She'd had great sex and lots of fun spending time with Emily, so why did she feel so unsettled?

Maybe I need more sex. Shaking her head, she moved closer and saw the blonde barrel racer talking to Duncan again. Lana paused, hesitating before approaching them.

"Come back to the motel with me, Duncan," Jennifer said. "It was good last time. Really good."

Lana heard, despite the chatter, and must have made a sound because Duncan's head jerked up.

"No, Jennifer," he said without taking his gaze off Lana.

"Why not?"

"Because he's with me." Lana hoped she wasn't stepping in where she wasn't wanted. He'd already said no. Duncan would realize she wanted to help him out and nothing more.

Just one more night of sex, she thought. *One more to tide me over for another year or so.*

"Oh, I thought...never mind." Tears filled Jennifer's eyes, and she turned away, pushing her way through the people loitering at the marquee entrance.

"I hope I didn't butt in and spoil things for you," Lana said.

"No. Your timing is perfect. Jennifer and I went out twice. Nothing serious. We're just friends."

"She was crying."

"I know. I don't understand why. It's a new trend," Duncan said, frowning after Jennifer. "I don't know what that was about because she knows we're friends and nothing more. Did you want something?"

No use prevaricating. Besides, if she didn't hurry, another woman might arrive to drag off Duncan. "I'm ready to go back to Saber and Emily's. I wondered if you'd like to come with me."

"Yes." Duncan took her hand and the anxious race of her heart settled. He hadn't hesitated.

"They say sex is good for a headache. I'm hoping that's true."

"So I'm gonna get lucky."

Lana snuck a quick glance at his face and couldn't discern his feelings on the situation. His mouth bore a slight grin though. She'd bet his mind floated in the gutter thinking about sex. Such a male thing to do. Sometimes she thought all Jamie had considered was sex and children. "I said so, didn't I?"

"No need to get testy," Duncan said, his hand in the small of her back as he guided her across the parking area to his SUV. The warmth of his touch crept through her body like a slowly unfurling streamer, gaining more impetus the longer his hand remained in contact. She shivered, wishing the silk wasn't between her skin and his touch, or better yet, that his lips caressed her flesh while a lone finger pumped into her aching channel.

"Sorry, I get a little snappy when I have a headache."

Duncan wondered if it was more than a headache. He'd heard her growl when Jennifer propositioned him, seen the annoyance flickering over her face. It had been a mere flash of emotion but it gave him hope. What her mind wanted and her body needed were two different things. She was fighting this thing between them so no wonder her head hurt.

He opened the door for her, closing it once she'd settled and rounded his vehicle to climb into the driver's seat.

"What time are you leaving for Queenstown tomorrow?"

"Emily asked me to stay for lunch. I haven't decided yet if I will or not."

Duncan calculated the hours until she left and knew it wasn't long enough. He needed a plan because from what he'd seen and heard from Emily and Saber, wooing Lana wasn't going to be easy. He started his vehicle and backed from the parking space, turning toward the road that led to the Mitchell homestead.

A glance at Lana told him her eyes were closed. Assuming she didn't want to talk, he took the time to put together a plan to win over Lana. His brow crinkled while he thought about and discarded possibilities. He kept coming back to the one idea that made his feline bristle and snarl with disapproval.

Romance.

Knowing Jamie, she hadn't experienced simple romance. Tonight he'd make love to her instead of enjoying simple sex. He'd show her with his body how much he cared for her and how much he wanted her. Once she returned to Queenstown, he'd drop by her restaurant and ask her for a date, send flowers for her reopening. If he asked, Emily would give him ideas. From what he knew of Emily, she took pleasure in helping others and gave good advice.

Yeah. Sounded like a plan to him. The time it took to win her over might chafe, but determination would prevail. If what she said was true, she didn't date and worked long hours. The lack of competition might work in his favor.

He pulled up outside the Mitchell homestead and switched off the ignition.

"Lana, are you awake? We're back," he said, stroking a finger across her soft cheek. Her eyes opened and heat bloomed in them, fiery green heat full of desire. Her pupils contracted to a black slit and a sultry purr rumbled in her throat.

"I've been dreaming about you, about sex."

In that moment Duncan knew his plan to romance her was the right way to go. A purist might suggest that having sharing a bed equated to putting sex first. Not so. Lust between a man and woman came in different packages. Duncan eagerly anticipated making love instead of aiming for simple pleasure.

"Good to know," he said. "Was it hot sex?"

Even in the dim light of his vehicle interior he caught the flush of her cheeks and grinned.

"It was good," she croaked, lifting a hand to wave in front of her face.

The transformation from purring kitten to flustered woman intrigued him and made him want to peel away the layers, to learn her on all the different levels. He inhaled on realizing this last, the thought bringing decision. In the past a woman had never fascinated him enough to make him want to get to know her, not after he'd walked away from Lana the first time. Yeah, it was strange the things a man learned about himself.

"How's the head?"

"Still achy, but not too bad. I'll be fine in the morning."

"I hope so."

Lana grinned and her face lit up in a way he hadn't seen since the first time he'd noticed her with Jamie. He shoved aside thoughts of his cousin and climbed out of his SUV. They met at the start of the path leading to the front door and linking hands they ambled hand in hand to the door.

Duncan came to a halt. "I left my gear bag in the SUV. Wait for me in the bedroom. I'll be right back." Leaving Lana, he loped back to his vehicle and grabbed a small daypack filled with a change of clothes. He hunted for the bottles of massage oil a physio had given him when he'd hurt his leg in a fall. Good. They were still in the side pocket. A massage could be romantic and he loved to touch Lana.

Triumphant, Duncan headed back to the house, taking both daypack and oils with him. He strode the dark passage to the bedroom Emily had allocated to Lana. She'd turned on a bedside lamp and light spilled from the bedroom into the passageway.

Lana's dress slithered downward, catching on her hips before whooshing to the floor. She stepped out of the circle of red silk, turning to face him when she heard his footsteps.

Duncan paused at the doorway. "God, you're stunning."

"And you're overdressed," she countered, sitting on the bed to unfasten her shoes. Seconds later she kicked them aside and stood again, sauntering over until she stopped in front of him.

His gaze dropped to her breasts and immediately he wanted to touch. Stick to the plan, he told himself. "Lie on the bed."

She obeyed, surprising the hell out of him.

"Facedown," he instructed.

She rolled over and his gaze drifted across the sexy line of her spine and the curve of her buttocks. Beautiful, and all his as long as he played this game right.

"Should I close my eyes?"

"Good idea, but don't go to sleep."

"Will you spank me if I disobey and nod off?"

Duncan considered it and couldn't restrain a smirk. "Did you like me spanking you?"

"Yes."

A simple and straightforward answer, her honesty brought a trace of pride and a smile. "I'm taking off my clothes. Won't be long." One boot clomped on the floor as he told her what he intended to do. "I'm saving spanking for special occasions," he said, seconds before his second boot hit the ground.

"Oh." She sounded disappointed, and he made a mental note of it. Although she'd fought his assertive tendencies she seemed to want them now. He'd have to think on the matter. Sex was one topic he didn't intend to discuss with Emily.

Duncan dragged off his clothes and rifled through the side pocket until his hand closed around a brown glass bottle of massage oil. Naked, he prowled over to the bed and straddled her hips.

"Are you awake, sweetheart?"

"Barely."

The physio he'd visited had given him two different bottles of oil. One lavender and the other reminded him of Oriental spices. Although the lavender one smelled more flowery and girly, he thought Lana would like the Oriental scent. He hoped he'd grabbed the right one.

"What are you going to do?"

His brows rose at the hint of uncertainty in her voice. "Scared?"

"No."

"Liar. I'll give you a massage and hopefully that will help the headache on its way."

"A massage?"

Duncan laughed at the sheer disbelief in her voice. Her tone said she wanted more, and it made the tension residing in the pit of his stomach disperse. Despite his impatience, his decision to give her time and romance seemed the right one. It might even be kinda fun. Sex had always come easy for him while Lana was making him work. All part of the cat-and-mouse game. Knowing Jamie, his cousin had rushed her into mating without a shred of romance. Not that he blamed Jamie since survival through mating was hardwired into the males—the need to have offspring and keep the species alive.

"Relax. You'll see. I'm good at this." He unscrewed the top and tipped a little oil on his hands before setting the bottle on the bedside cabinet to avoid spills. The scent of spices tinged with a hint of exotic flowers rose to meet him and he gave a silent grunt of satisfaction. After dispersing the oil across his palms, he glided his hands over her back, varying the firmness and speed of the strokes just as his physio had instructed him.

A silent laugh filled him when he remembered his complaints about having a massage and how the other cowboys gave him a hard time. He'd come to appreciate the benefits and cajoled the physio into giving him some hints so he could incorporate massage into his sex life. Maybe it was a feline thing with all the stroking. Duncan couldn't think of anything better than touches and caresses, unless good sex followed. His cock filled at the thought of plunging into Lana's snug pussy. Yeah. Good times ahead.

First the massage. Duncan alternated firm strokes with finger-light ones where he traced patterns on her back. Her soft groan of pleasure resounded right through him as he worked down her body. He kneaded the curves of her bottom, using deeper pressure and the tension seeped from her before working up again to rub her back, neck and shoulders.

"Your skin is so soft."

Her incoherent mumble made him smile.

"I'll do the talking. It's not often we males can get a word in."

She snorted, not moving, and he grinned, enjoying himself. Touching and spending time with Lana was as good as the sex. It seemed romance worked for him too.

"Hmm, what should we discuss? I'd like to know more about your restaurant. We'll leave that for another time when it's easier for you to talk. What if I tell you about Hawaii? I had a holiday there before I headed home. I loved it all. The water is this bright blue color. It's different from our water here. Our sea always looks moody while the tropical waters sparkle with happiness. Sounds corny, I know, yet it's true."

Although Lana didn't comment, he sensed her interest and continued talking while he rubbed and fondled her body, his hands gliding easily with the oil.

"There's white sand and coconut palms right on the beach at Waikiki. When you travel inland the land is green and mountainous. Some of the islands are dry on one side with verdant green on the other and steep, towering cliffs that meet the sea. One day I'll take you there. Turn over for me, and I'll do your front." He moved so she could roll over.

"I want to travel one day. It won't be for a long time until I pay off more of my mortgage."

"Shush. Relax," Duncan said. Instinct told him to bite back on his urge to offer her money. He understood pride and refused to trample hers. His parents hadn't understood his desire to go into rodeo, wanting him to work on the family farm in Northern Canterbury. It had been a point of pride and sheer bloody orneriness that he succeeded on his own and made a decent living without accepting financial help from his parents. Yeah, he understood pride and admired Lana's determination.

Duncan reached over for more oil and hoped Emily wouldn't mind if the duvet cover suffered. Somehow he thought she'd take it in stride. When he moved back over Lana, her eyes were open and she was frowning.

"You're meant to be relaxing," he chided, taking pleasure in looking at her form. Although her breasts tempted him, he moved down the bed to start work on her feet and legs, gliding hands over the contours and muscles beneath his fingers.

The purring sound coming from deep in Lana's chest brought both a smile and satisfaction. Duncan worked up her thighs, massaging the soft inner skin with deep thumb pressure. Her body gleamed under his ministrations, the oil shining and highlighting her sleek musculature.

"Do you get a chance to run in feline form often?"

"No. Until the other day I hadn't shifted for months."

Duncan glanced at her in concern. "It's better for your health if you can shift regularly."

Lana bit her lip, and after meeting his eyes for an instant, let her lids flutter closed. "I know. It's not always easy."

Another thing to add to his romance plan—the temptation of a run on private land. He worked his way up toward the genital area without touching her intimately. That would come later. He glided his hands over her torso, ignoring her breasts, merely sliding his fingers around them. Her breathing became slower, deeper, and Duncan sensed the tension seep from her muscles during the prolonged touching session.

"I've been lucky enough to go for runs on a regular basis. It helps keep me fit and strong. The bulls sense my feline and it makes them harder to ride, although I've learned a few things about disguising my scent over the years."

"I—"

"No talking." Duncan massaged her face before removing the combs and clips from her hair and running his fingers across her scalp.

Her eyes popped open to snare his gaze. "You want me. Your arousal tells me that."

"Yes," Duncan said, his eyes crinkling into a smile. "Did my erection give you a few clues?"

"It helped, and the heat coming off you is incredible. Your musk is rising too."

All true. He ached for her, although he enjoyed touching her pliant body too much to hurry the process of seduction. "I'm not the only one who's enjoying all this touching."

"I never have time to relax."

Duncan nodded, understanding more than what she was telling him. No one had spoiled or indulged her before. Maybe she hadn't let anyone close enough, despite being married. That would change, and the idea he'd make the difference made his heart clench. It seemed he'd learned things about himself tonight. He needed romance as much as she did. Duncan glided a hand over her hip before pouring more oil into the palm of his hand. Eventually, Lana would let him in and trust him enough to mention her marriage to Jamie. Soon they'd be mates.

Gradually Duncan moved his attention to her breasts, squeezing the plump curves and moving closer and closer to her nipples. Finally, he grasped each one between fingers and thumbs and tugged while watching Lana's face.

The delicate flush of arousal suffused her cheeks, making her eyes darken and the pupils contract to feline slits. He replaced his fingers with his mouth, drawing one nipple inside while he drew aimless shapes on her other breast with his fingers. They smoothed across her oil-slicked skin, her arousal combining with the spicy oil. Lana's soft purrs and the subtle arching of her body brought satisfaction and pleasure.

"So responsive," he murmured. "I like that." Duncan dipped his head and dragged his tongue past her cleavage, enjoying the rasp against her flesh. The flavor of the oil—not so much. "Ugh, next time remind me to choose an oil that tastes better."

Lana laughed at him. "It might taste horrid but imagine the way our skin will slide together, all slippery and sleek."

"Like this?" Duncan rubbed his chest against her breasts and reached up to kiss her. Their lips came together in a soft, barely there caress, gradually deepening. A slow and easy kiss with a hint of promise and hunger. The touch sizzled through his bloodstream, coming to a halt in his cock. When he lifted his head, his heart raced. "Damn, that has to be the sexiest kiss I've ever had."

"Do it again."

"Something tells me she liked it."

A growl rumbled from Lana and she grabbed him by the ears. "Ow."

"Kiss me quick." Lana puckered up.

Smirking, Duncan grasped her shoulders and rolled so she ended on top of him. Their lips met in another gentle encounter, the slide of tongues like a waltz into greater pleasure. When they pulled apart, they were both breathing hard, the scent of Oriental oil filling the air. Duncan ran his hand over her head, tangling fingers in her dark hair. Each time they came together the urge to mate increased, the mating heat rising within him. He eyed the fleshy part of her shoulder where it met her neck and his canines pushed through his gums. The words trembled on his lips and he knew he had to bite them back, leaving them unsaid or he'd lose her.

"Ride me," he said. He'd intended to make love to her, using every bit of his finesse and experience. Instead a tremble sped through him, his feline riding him hard.

"My pleasure." Lana pushed up and straddled his hips. In her scramble for position she flashed her sex and a shot of desire hit him.

"You want me." Satisfaction coated his words.

"I told you earlier I hadn't had sex since Jamie died."

The hard set of her mouth drew his attention and questions. They remained unasked. It wasn't the right time. Instead he watched her, searching for clues. "I won't have sex again for a while because I'll be busy. I want you to fuck me so bad right now that I'll beg if you tell me to stop."

His feline surged to the fore, knowledge he was the only one since Jamie pushing past his control. Duncan had her under his body in one swift move, moving between her legs and sliding home before she could blink. Once fully seated, he stilled, each breath coming in a roar. His gaze dropped to the special place on her shoulder and he rasped his tongue across the spot. Back and forth. Back and forth. Her pulse jumped, and she gasped a quick intake of air. Duncan opened his mouth and scraped his teeth across her skin, teasing her and pushing harder at his control.

"Don't," she whispered.

Duncan lifted his head. "I'd never mark you without your agreement." His canines made his husky voice emerge with a slight lisp.

Lana nodded despite the wariness in her eyes.

"I'd never trap you." He scowled when she didn't respond, pissed at her for doubting his integrity. "Although we didn't use protection yesterday. You don't think I'll expect close contact if we have a child?"

"I'm protected. I'm on the Pill."

Duncan's eyes closed for an instant, and until that moment he hadn't realized how much he'd welcome a child into his life. Lana's child. "Good," he said. "Good to know." Damn. Disappointment clawed at his gut. He shoved it away. *Don't blow your chance.*

He pulled out and pushed back into her moist flesh. Using controlled movements, he built the simmering pleasure higher, relieved when he saw Lana's eyes flicker closed. The last thing he wanted right now was for her to see his emotions when they were so close to the surface, his control a mere façade.

"Yes," she whispered, clutching his shoulders and hanging on tight.

Gradually he upped the pace until his cock slammed into her in choppy strokes. When her tongue curled out to lick her lips, he kissed her. Although he tried to keep it gentle, she wouldn't let him. Her sex flexed and gripped his cock. His balls drew tight, and after one more thrust, he lost control. An almost pained groan hissed past his protruding canines and when he stilled, embedded in her pussy, the sharp contractions of his cock prolonged the pleasure.

Lana panted beneath him, making him aware his weight was resting on her. Lifting to his elbows, he pressed kisses to her face, moving again and hoping to give her enough friction to come. "Touch yourself," he whispered against her ear. "I want to watch your face when you come."

He thrust again but his cock softened, and no wonder considering the force with which he'd come.

Lana licked her lips, and he watched the move avidly, fascinated by the want reflected in her face. Her beautiful eyes glowed and a soft flush covered her chest. As he watched, she slipped a hand between their bodies.

"I need more," she said.

Duncan bit back a laugh and pulled away. "Let's do it this way," he said, pushing two fingers inside her wet pussy. Knocking her finger aside, he dipped his head and licked around her swollen clit. Her body bucked and her sex squeezed his fingers.

"Yes," she said, half moaning the word. "Again."

Duncan smiled against her flesh, amused at her bossiness. At least she didn't seem angry that he'd come and she hadn't. He settled in to push her into pleasure, hopefully as great as he'd experienced.

Lana melted into the mattress, relaxed and mellow even though she had a man licking her private parts. For a while she watched him, scanning his hair and profile, the flash of his tongue. Her decision to have a weekend of sex and to spend one more night with Duncan had been the best male-related resolve she'd made for a long time.

Letting her eyes fall closed, she concentrated on the sensations. The man had a talented tongue. It dragged across her flesh, rough and abrasive—a luscious tug that pulled at her clit and transmitted a tingle of pleasure through her abdomen and down her legs. With each lick the feelings intensified, and she lifted into his face, silently urging him to give her more pressure, more drag. Just more.

Duncan's fingers curved with each thrust and he began a direct assault on her clit. Instead of licking around, his tongue moved across every second or third lick. His strokes varied so she never knew to expect. Not that it mattered. This man knew his way around a woman's body. It should've bothered her—heck, it might later—but right now she was busy enjoying the hell out of his experience. A gasp escaped, sounding so much like a purr, she bit her bottom lip to halt the sounds.

Duncan stopped and lifted his head. "You're a feline. You don't have to hold back on my account. I love your sexy purrs."

Lana gave a jerky nod. "Don't stop." Heck, if the man didn't start again, she might commit murder. Either that or lock herself in the bathroom and take care of things herself.

"No way, sweetheart. I'm enjoying myself."

Thankfully, he returned to the task with delicate precision. After three tense seconds she relaxed again, the feel-good sensations creeping back. Duncan pushed her harder, and she purred, the pleasure streaking from her clit and down her legs in a fireball. She groaned, riding out the climax, her pussy contracting on his fingers. An earthquake. That was what it was. Duncan gave her clit another lick and a second, almost painful series of spasms sped through her.

He dragged his fingers from her body and moved up the bed until they were face-to-face.

"You are so beautiful." The husky rumble of his voice held satisfaction. Normally she'd inform him he had a big head and chop him down to size. Right now every muscle sang a relaxed tune. Difficult to summon the energy.

"You taste good." Duncan watched her as he licked her juices from his fingers. He held her gaze, his eyes dark, swirling with passion. Just as well she intended to head back to Queenstown tomorrow and wouldn't see Duncan for months. In two short days she'd grown addicted to his lovemaking. Greedily she craved more. An impossibility. Tomorrow, she returned to work, and he'd be nothing more than a good memory. Her lips lifted in a grin. A perfect memory.

"Something funny?" He smoothed the hair from her face and tucked it behind her ear.

"No, not at all," she said, sobering. "I'm tired. You should go back to the campground."

"I'm tired as well and I'd like to stay."

Lana opened her mouth to object as he climbed from the bed and turned out the light. On his return, the mattress depressed with his weight. Sighing because she didn't want him to go, she turned on her side. He moved behind her, tugging her against his chest, a possessive hand curving around her waist. The nonsexual comfort made her sigh again. Really, she should protest. But she remained silent, telling herself tomorrow would be soon enough to part. She'd had great sex and felt better than she had for months. No need to end the weekend on an argument when they could part on good terms tomorrow.

Chapter 7

Farmer Duncan

L ana walked through her gutted restaurant and tried not to panic. The builders had assured her they'd finish by the opening on Monday the following week. It was only two weeks late. She inhaled and at once wished she hadn't. A sneeze erupted. Lana breathed through her mouth. A fresh plaster stench, varnish and paint swirled through the air, odors that hadn't been present the previous day. Queasiness lurched through her stomach at the consequences of remaining closed for another extra week. Thank goodness she could see progress, even if her feline side hated the stench.

A knock on the door dragged her attention from her remodeling problems.

"Richard, have you come to see the mess?" Lana greeted the lawyer from next door.

"I thought they'd be further along than this," he said, coming to stand beside her.

"A problem with staff. You know the flu bug going around? Well, it decimated the builder's team. I wanted to fire his ass until I realized he'd dragged himself out of bed to work on my renovations. He looked so sick I sent him home."

"You're too soft," Richard murmured. "Let me take care of it for you. I'll get them to finish the work and sue them for loss of income."

Lana hid her irritation behind a quick frown. No wonder things hadn't worked between them from her perspective. Take-charge men who thought they knew better pissed her off. "Thanks, I appreciate the offer. I've dealt with it."

"Let me sue him on your behalf."

"We've worked out a deal. Yes, he's inconvenienced me. It couldn't be helped. Business is light anyway since the stupid flu has struck so many people." Lana held up a hand when Richard started to speak again. She'd been right to keep their relationship on a business footing.

Her thoughts drifted to Duncan, as they often did, even though she'd tried to stomp on the bad habit. What would he recommend her to do? Or would he try to take over as well?

"No, Richard. Everything is fine. I have several private parties booked. Once I reopen everything will revert to normal."

"I came by to take you out for a drink. Are you ready to go?"

Once again his pure disregard for her feelings—on any subject—grated. Perhaps she'd like him to ask instead of tell. The man didn't have a clue. "No, I have things to do here. The Goods and Services return has to go out in the mail tonight."

She'd tried to attack it yesterday but illness had felled her, and she'd dragged herself upstairs to her apartment above the restaurant. This morning she'd felt better, at least until she entered the restaurant, so the paint rather than the flu had caused her queasiness.

"Are you brushing me off?"

Surprised, Lana turned to him. "What are you talking about? I have to do my bookwork tonight."

"I'll ask Marjorie from the dress shop out for a drink."

Lana rolled her eyes. What did he expect her to do? Beg him not to take Marjorie? Lana went for nonconfrontational despite wanting to flay him with the blunt truth. "I'm sure she'd enjoy a drink with you." Perhaps Richard's strange behavior was due to impending flu. She caught him staring at her lips and the lustful look jolted her right to her stomach. It wasn't a pleasurable sensation, not when she compared him to Duncan. "I'll see you tomorrow, Richard."

With a curt nod he left, the door clanging shut after him. Talk about weird. Shaking her head at the silliness of men, Lana did a final walk-through, checking the progress of the day while trying to ignore the unsettled lurching of her stomach. The builder had promised his crew would be here at six in the morning. Her sleep might suffer, but it was a small price if they finished the alterations. The sooner she could get rid of the paint and varnish smell, the quicker her feline would settle. Sometimes, the feline's excellent scent receptors didn't merge well with city life.

125

Someone tapped on the door and she grouchily whirled to face her visitor, ready to tell them to go away. The urge faded on seeing him. *Duncan*. Her heart slammed against her ribs as she gestured for him to come inside. What was he doing here? And worst of all why was she so thrilled to see him? That was the kicker.

"Hey, Lana. Whoa!" He paused, his nose wrinkling. "That smell is horrendous. Can I coerce you into coming out for dinner or a drink?"

"What are you doing here? I thought you'd be at a rodeo somewhere." She scanned him from head to foot, checking for injuries, relief bringing lightheadedness. Nothing obvious. His strong, muscular body looked as sexy as usual and did the normal number on her knees. Stupid hormones.

"That's part of what I wanted to discuss. Please, I hate this smell. Isn't there a pub on the corner?"

Lana laughed. "The smell isn't the best. Okay, a quick drink. I have office work I need to finish so I can't be away for long." She grabbed her wallet and hurried to join him, pausing to lock up and pocket the keys.

"Where's the best place for a drink?" Duncan asked.

"The pub you saw on the corner will work. I often have a drink there with friends." Lana craved a kiss. Badly. The urge to touch simmered through her like a compulsion. She inhaled, pulling his seductive scent into her lungs. He beat the stench of the paint by a wide mile.

"Let's go." Duncan took her hand and her breath exited in a whoosh. She'd spent two nights with him, and seeing him now, she realized how much she'd missed him, how there were a million little details about her days she'd stored up to tell him. The thought shocked her because that was exactly what she'd done with Jamie, or at least until he'd started to resent her restaurant because he wanted her to stay home and have babies.

"Why are you here?" she repeated.

"I've retired."

Her mouth dropped open in shock. "But you love the rodeo and you're good at it."

"I wanted to try something else. Despite healing well, even a feline can take only so many falls." Duncan pushed the door to the pub open and ushered her inside. "Want a glass of wine?"

"Please. I'll grab a table." Lana saw Richard standing at the bar with Marjorie and grimaced. Great. That was all she needed. He'd think she lied to him. Coming to a quick decision, she crossed the tiled floor to say hello instead of following her initial impulse to hide. "A friend dropped by after you left, Richard, and twisted my arm. Hi, Marjorie. How's business?"

"Slow," the brunette said. "I'm hoping it will improve. This flu seems to have hit the tourists too. When are you reopening?"

"Next week, all going well."

"Good. Your coffee is so much better and I've been dying to have a piece of that caramel slice you make."

"I'll make a batch on opening day. See you later," Lana said to both of them.

"Aren't you going to introduce your friend?" Richard's jaw stuck out in a pugnacious manner.

Lana kept her smile intact despite his snide tone. "Sure. We're only here for a quick drink because I still have that GST return to do before tomorrow." Lana sensed rather than saw Duncan behind her. "Richard, Marjorie, this is my husband's cousin Duncan."

Duncan set the drinks on the bar and stepped forward to offer his hand. "Pleased to meet you."

"Oh, a cousin," Richard said, his shoulders visibly relaxing.

Lana wanted to hit him. His behavior had reached peculiar, almost as if he thought she belonged to him. Never. Not in this lifetime.

"We're not related," Duncan said.

Richard's smile faded, and Lana had to work extra hard to maintain hers while Marjorie and Duncan chatted.

Finally Lana decided she'd suffered enough torture. Besides, Duncan had roused her curiosity. "I'll see you at the opening next week," she said.

"If not before," Richard said.

Not if she saw him first. With a curt nod, Lana walked away at Duncan's side. They took possession of a secluded corner table out of sight of Richard and Marjorie.

"Boyfriend?" Duncan asked.

"We've been out to dinner a few times." Lana hated the defensive note in her voice. It was none of Duncan's business.

"He wants more."

"And I'm not interested. I have more important things to do." So there! She'd told him. Lana reached for her wine, disturbed to find her hand trembling. "What are you going to do now?"

"I've bought a parcel of land not far from Cromwell. I intend to breed bulls for the South Island rodeo circuit, and after talking to Saber, I intend to dabble in grapes. They need more land for planting and I have it. Later on I might start a school to help train younger bull riders."

"Oh." It was all she could say. Inside, emotions rioted through her. Excitement. Alarm. And sex—she contemplated that too. One weekend hadn't been enough to sate her craving for the physical outlet of sex. Lana glanced at Duncan and blushed at his intent regard. Desire spread, tugging at her breasts and tingles surged through her lower belly. A need for sex after a long drought. Nothing to worry about.

"Is that your only comment?"

"Wow. I'm...it's unexpected. Of course I'm excited for you. Have you taken possession of the land yet? When did this happen? When did you decide to change directions?"

"I moved in last weekend."

"And? Are you living there?" She'd see Duncan again, and he might be willing to share a bed on occasion. The idea put a brake on her thoughts. They didn't have a future. Thinking of a relationship had landed her in trouble last time. Despite loving Jamie, the knowledge they'd grown apart gnawed at her. They might have ended up hating each other if they'd continued on the path they'd traveled.

"There's a house on the property. Nothing flash, but I intend to work on improvements when I have time. You should see the land." His eyes sparkled with enthusiasm. "There are acres of rolling hills and a stream runs through for water. Even at the height of summer there's plenty of water for cattle."

"A man with a dream." The tight bands of anxiety loosened around Lana's chest. She recognized the signs of ambition and determination since she bore the traits herself. And if he intended to work on the farm, he wouldn't have time to bother her. "You didn't say when you decided to go into farming."

"I've been considering it for a while," Duncan said, picking up his handle of beer to take a sip. "I waited for the sale to go through before I told anyone."

Lana nodded, relaxing for the first time in the last two weeks. She leaned back into the squishy leather chair and drank her wine, comfortable with the silence that had fallen between them.

"Come back to my place with me tonight?"

Lana jolted, sending splashes of her wine flying before she could set her glass on the wooden-topped table sitting between them. *Yes, she'd love to.* "I don't think so." Good grief! What was she thinking? The paint fumes must have damaged a few brain cells.

"Why not? If your quarters are above the restaurant, won't they smell of paint and varnish?"

"Yes, except I need to complete my GST return tonight." It wasn't an excuse, dammit. She needed to do her return.

"Bring your bookwork with you."

"You wouldn't mind if I did office work instead of paying attention to you?"

Duncan shrugged. "Why would I? I understand you have responsibilities. Besides, it won't take the entire night to do the return. You could do it while I cook dinner."

Lana's mouth opened and closed a few times while she tried to decide on her reply. Shock tinged her thoughts. Duncan was offering to cook? Offering to give her time alone to do her bookwork?

"As long as you're sure," she said. Jamie had hated her doing anything that took her attention from him. Her work had become a sore subject, and she'd found it easier to cede to his wishes, saving an argument and days of uncomfortable silence.

"I'm sure. Do you want another drink or are you ready to leave?"

"I'm ready to go now," Lana said. "It won't take long to grab my laptop and the folders of paperwork."

"What time do you need to be back in the morning?"

"The builders are coming around six. I've spoken with the foreman and they have a key."

"I can have you back at ten. Is that okay?"

"Perfect. I could drive out to save you coming back."

"I have to come back tomorrow to pick up an order of farm equipment. There's no point taking your vehicle too."

Lana shrugged, her pulse racing faster at spending time with Duncan even though her brain screamed of danger. Suddenly her eyes narrowed on him. "I'm not interested in a relationship."

"Who mentioned a relationship? I want to spend a few hours with a friend. The farm will keep me busy. I figured if we were both free we could spend time together."

A frown creased her brow while she considered Duncan's words. "What did you have in mind?" She didn't try to hide her suspicions.

"A meal together. A movie. Think you could handle that?"

Even though his mouth hadn't quirked into even the faintest grin and his eyes appeared somber, his amusement shimmered in the air. "Aren't you scared I'll get the wrong idea? Want more than you're prepared to give?"

Duncan had to work hard not to laugh aloud. She'd run a mile if he admitted he wanted her any way he could have her. No, since he required a more subtle game, he intended to woo her, play the long game. He had ideas all right, but he was a patient man. "I'm not worried. You've told me you want to grow your business and I understand because I want to do the same thing for mine." They'd be together soon. He sensed it in his gut, and the weekend in her bed had solidified his plan. Spending time with her and not pushing would help build trust. Yeah, he'd sneak up and pounce before she grasped the danger.

"Oh. That's okay then."

Half an hour later Duncan drove through the outskirts of Queenstown and away from the narrow lake framed by The Remarkables mountain range. The journey took them through the Kawarau gorge to the Gibbston Valley with its acres of vineyards.

"That's the Mitchell vineyard," Duncan said, pointing to a group of buildings on the left dominated by one with a soaring roof.

"The shape reminds me of a bird in flight."

"Yeah, Leo told me they've won design awards with the design."

Lana nodded. "Now that I know the Mitchells own it I might make a point of stopping."

Duncan wanted to say he'd take her but remained silent, not wanting to push too hard. "It's not far to my place. Another fifteen minutes." It was the damnedest thing—the nerves simmering in his stomach. He wanted Lana to like his farm.

He turned onto a side road and took the second left, driving down a long, winding gravel road before pulling up outside a bungalow-style house. Duncan had plans for the house and grounds, and while they needed work, the view was spectacular.

"Wow." Lana scrambled from his vehicle and walked around to join him. "It's a beautiful setting."

Pride rose in Duncan along with contentment. He slung his arm around her shoulders and hugged Lana to his side. "I'm pleased with it."

"What's not to like?" Lana scoffed. "The rolling hills, the mountains in the distance. The river and the grapevines. It looks as if you could shift and run for miles without running into any humans."

"How does a run now sound? It's not dark for a couple of hours."

"I'd love it." Her eyes sparkled, and although he'd considered hustling Lana inside to show her his bedroom, a run excited her so much waiting seemed a small price to pay.

"What about your GST return?"

Lana wrinkled her nose. "A run will clear my head. I should complete the return in no time."

Duncan stepped away from her and unfastened the buttons on his shirt.

"What are you doing?"

"I thought you wanted to go for a run." Duncan liked the way Lana's gaze dropped to his chest and had to bite back a groan when she licked her lips.

"I do."

He tossed the shirt aside and bent to unlace his boots. He undid the button and zipper of his jeans, removing his boxers and socks to toss them in a heap. Naked, he turned to Lana. "Something wrong?"

"Ah no."

Grinning, he pictured the feline in his mind and let the shift take him. He had her hooked. Now all he needed to do was reel her in.

Chapter 8

Togetherness

"I enjoyed the run so much," Lana said, scooping her clothes off the ground. "I love your farm. The land is beautiful."

Duncan nodded, gathering his own clothes and boots. "This plot spoke to me the first time I visited. Go take a shower and do your bookwork while I take care of dinner."

Lana stopped walking. "Really?"

"Yeah, that way we can spend the rest of the night relaxing." And doing more, he hoped. He scanned the part of her chest visible above the clothes she clutched. Damn, he wanted her. He opened the front door and stood aside to let her enter first. "Last door on the right is the bathroom. My bedroom is on the left."

"Are we sleeping together?"

"If that's what you want." His breath caught while he waited for her reply.

"I want," she said before sashaying away and disappearing into the bathroom.

Duncan dropped his boots by the door and grinned. After dressing, he turned and padded barefoot into the kitchen. He was gonna get lucky tonight. Until now he hadn't been sure. After opening the battered fridge, he grabbed the bacon and egg pie Emily had sent for him. Saber had dropped it off when he'd gone to visit the family vineyard. Duncan turned on the oven and while he waited for it to heat, he made a lettuce salad to go with the bean salad Emily had also packed. Lana came into the kitchen with her laptop and two folders of invoices, settling with minimum of fuss to her bookwork.

While he worked on dinner, he glanced at her a couple of times, enjoying her presence, her feminine scent and the view she presented seated at his table.

His. His feline stirred in a reproachful protest. Duncan tamped him down, determined to work to his slow and steady plan. The cat-and-mouse thing and the skillful chase had gone well so far. It wouldn't do to screw up his hard work by letting his feline take control.

The phone rang and Duncan strode over to the kitchen counter to grab the receiver. "Hello."

"Hi, Duncan."

Jennifer. The woman was becoming a real pain in the ass. With a scowl, Duncan walked into another room and hoped Lana didn't try to eavesdrop. "What can I do for you?"

"Duncan," Jennifer chided. "I thought you'd be pleased to hear from me. From what I hear you've been working hard on that new farm of yours. When are you inviting me to visit?"

"I'm busy and not set up for guests," Duncan said. "Besides, aren't you following the circuit?"

"No, I'm home since Cricket injured his leg during training. The vet says I need to rest him for a month."

"I thought you had two horses." Blast the woman. How had she found his number? He decided not to make a big deal about it.

"I do, except I only took Cricket with me this time. I thought I'd give you a ring to say hello and see if we could get together."

Damn. "There's someone else," Duncan said.

"That woman from the dance?"

"That's right."

"Oh, I thought she was your cousin."

"No," he said, leaving it at that. The less he told her the better. "I have to go. Good luck with Cricket." Duncan hung up and returned to the kitchen to check the pie, his gut uneasy.

"Trouble?" Lana asked, her fingers tapping over the keys before studying him.

"One of the barrel racer girls. She keeps ringing me."

"Uh-oh. Woman trouble." Lana smiled brightly, dragging his focus to her lips. Plump and pink, he knew of their softness. The knowledge didn't stop him craving a taste. So far they'd touched in a casual manner. He'd wanted to keep things light, so he didn't frighten her. A mistake. He needed more.

SHELLEY MUNRO

"I told her I wasn't interested."

"Probably the best thing to do," Lana said. "That pie smells good. Did you make it?"

"Emily sent it with Saber. He dropped in this morning on the way to the vineyard."

"Emily is a great cook. I've finished. It didn't take me as long as I thought to update the cashbook. Should I set the table?"

"Thanks. Cutlery is in this drawer. Plates are in the cupboard near the pantry."

Duncan caught Lana checking him out and smirked inside, letting the sensual tension build. Her subtle interest made him even more certain of his plan. He pulled a bottle of Sauvignon Blanc from the fridge and opened it before retrieving glasses from the cupboard.

The meal together, the casual chat about Middlemarch, his farm and her restaurant made Duncan visualize the future. He liked the concept, especially when Lana played footsie under the table. Her laugh tinkled between them, her green eyes crinkling at the corners when she stroked her toe across his groin.

"You should take care," he warned.

"Or what? Someone will spank my bottom?"

"You like that too much."

Her face flushed and he couldn't restrain a grin. He'd never experienced this easy give-and-take with a woman before, not without an alarm blaring, warning him to back off. He'd seen it between Saber and Emily, but had never wanted or sought it on his own behalf.

138

Lana stroked her toes up his inner thigh and rubbed across his stirring cock. "What will you do to me?"

"I'll tie you to my bed and pleasure you, pushing you to the edge until you're begging for release." Nothing less than the truth. He'd thought of doing this, exerting more of his personality in the bedroom now that they were more comfortable together. If she wanted to give him an opportunity to indulge, he was ready.

"You've threatened that before."

"Promised," he corrected. "There's a world of difference."

"I see." Lana stroked her foot across his lap.

A quick downward glance showed toenails painted a delicate pink. "Go to the bedroom. Take off your clothes and lie on the bed to wait for me." When she stared, her lips parting in surprise, he lifted her feet from his lap, pushed away from the table and stood. "In the bedroom. Now."

Lana stood, a slight crease furrowing her brow. "What are you going to do with me?"

Duncan cleared the table. "Do you trust me?"

"Yes."

"Then do what I say."

Still frowning, she turned away and walked to the doorway leading to the passage. Duncan caught her glancing over her shoulder, although pretended not to notice, continuing with his tasks. The retreating footsteps and the tiny huff of pique brought a grin. Lana amused him. He waited for fifteen minutes, washing the dishes first before he followed Lana to his bedroom. He'd wanted her to think and wonder what he might do to her, start the slow buildup to arousal.

Eager to see her on his bed, his footsteps hastened. He came to a halt at the doorway and scowled, although inside amusement bubbled, wanting to free itself in a wide grin. "I thought I told you to take off your clothes, lie on the bed and wait for me." His bottom lip quivered while he bit back the threatening wave of humor. "I didn't tell you to start without me."

Lana paused, her brows rising. Then she continued with the languid stroking between her legs, unashamedly flashing her pussy between strokes. "You were taking too long. I thought I'd get warmed up."

Duncan watched the measured moves of her hand as she stroked her glistening folds and teased her clit. He stepped into the bedroom, fighting a laugh. "Hands above your head. Now."

"I haven't finished."

Duncan rounded a pile of unpacked boxes and crossed to her side. The bed was the only piece of furniture in the room and dominated the space. A plain green duvet covered the mattress, the sheets a paler shade of mint. He'd chosen them because the color reminded him of Lana's eyes. "Hands above your head," he repeated, his tone brooking no-nonsense.

Pouting, she stroked across her clit one final time before removing her hand and raising both above her head. "Well, this is boring."

Duncan let his eyes drift over her naked body from her pink-tipped toenails, up her toned legs and naked pussy, along her flat belly and rib cage to her plump breasts. Finally he met her jade-green eyes and smiled. "It's not boring from this end."

"Humph."

He strode to the wardrobe and pulled out several lengths of hemp rope. Using a larks head knot, he bound one wrist, taking care to allow a finger's width of give. The last thing he wanted was to hurt her. Duncan tied her other hand and moved to the end of the bed to tie her ankles. "Basic rules. We'll work on a traffic light system. Green for go, amber for caution or slow down, red for stop. You're in control of when we start and stop. Okay?"

Lana chewed on her bottom lip, the move a giveaway of her nervousness. "What exactly are you going to do?"

"Pleasure you."

"Then why do I need a safe word?"

"If your arms or legs go to sleep because I've tied you too tight or if something I do, some way I touch you is painful rather than giving you pleasure and you don't enjoy it, you need a way out. You're giving control over to me, and that takes a certain amount of trust. Your trust is precious and I'd never abuse it. A safe word is part of that trust."

A tiny frown appeared then cleared. "Okay."

"Good." He looped the hemp rope around one ankle and tied it with competent moves, repeating the tie on her other ankle. "Comfortable? Are any of the knots rubbing?" Duncan watched while Lana tested them.

"Um, what if there's a fire or something?"

"You'll shock the hell out of the volunteer fire brigade." Duncan laughed. "I know my knots and can unfasten them quickly. My bag of toys contains a pair of clippers in case of emergency."

"I'm feeling vulnerable."

"There's no need. This is about pleasure." Duncan moved up to the top of the bed and leaned over to caress her upper arm. She shivered, her eyelids fluttering closed. A soft sigh escaped her. His cock jumped, pressing against his fly. "I'm taking my clothes off now."

Her lips curled upward. "Are you hinting I should watch?"

"I'm telling you to watch."

Tension choked the room as she lifted her eyelids to focus on him. A ragged breath caused his cock to jerk again. Without haste he unbuttoned his shirt, slid it off his shoulders. His gaze caught hers and held it with hot intent. The cotton shirt dropped to the floor with a whisper. He unfastened the button on his jeans and slid down the zipper. Lana stared at his groin, her concentration total. Blood pumped through his body as her gaze stroked his body. His feline growled, pushing for release. Canine teeth pushed into his mouth and when he tugged the denim over his hips, dark claws were visible beneath his fingernails.

"Come closer," she murmured.

"I'm in charge, babe." Duncan maneuvered his boxers over his erection and stepped out of them.

Lana watched him stalk closer to the bed and her heart lurched, the sensation almost painful. Her feline rode her hard, protesting the restraints on her wrists and ankles. She stirred, shifting her weight. The way he looked at her, as if she were precious and important, made the blood pound through her veins. He leaned over and she swallowed, her throat and mouth suddenly parched. His fingers trailed over her shoulder and her arm, a light touch, but enough to send a shiver speeding across her skin. Prickles of sensation collected at the juncture of her thighs while her nipples pulled tight.

She imagined the ways he could touch her, the things he could do to her. The pleasure and a tad of pain. She imagined this and molten desire simmered to life. He ran his fingers over her collarbone and bent to lick around her bellybutton. Each of his touches remained innocent yet she quivered, straining against the ropes and into his touch.

"That's so good."

Duncan smiled, and she caught a flash of sharp canines. The knowledge he was so fully involved, enough for his slumbering feline to exert even the smallest amount of control, elevated her pleasure.

A stroke of his hand across her rib cage brought a quiver, the brush of his lips on her inner thigh made her sigh. The mattress moved when he stood and she watched his graceful saunter across the floor to the wardrobe. He grabbed a battered leather bag and brought it back to the bed.

SHELLEY MUNRO

"Close your eyes."

Like an obedient child, she did. Despite being the one tied, she drifted into a different world where Duncan handled her pleasure. Weird. Giving control to him was kind of liberating. She sensed he moved closer, and she waited, a prickle of anticipation dancing through the pit of her stomach.

Something soft and silky brushed her upper arm and glided over the curve of one breast. Her skin became supersensitive, and every sense intensified. She smelled Duncan's soap and the crisp cotton of the duvet beneath her body. Lana heard his steady breathing and the rustle of the bedclothes, the faint creak of the ropes when she flexed her muscles. He kept her guessing. She was never sure where he'd touch next or whether it would be with his fingertips or the thing she'd identified as a brush. Gradually his touches became more intimate, a graze of her nipples, a brush over her lips and the faint teasing strokes over her folds.

Vaguely she heard his murmurs of praise as she sank deeper into her newfound world of pleasure and serenity. Duncan shifted position, and seconds later, the stroke of a tongue down her cleft added to the kaleidoscope of sensations. A finger smoothed lower, gliding, pressing. Nerves sprang to life. Her pussy moistened and her breasts swelled.

"Perfect," Duncan said in praise. His husky voice brought satisfaction as she drifted, the layering of sensations both intense and surprising. She thought she'd known her body, known her capabilities, but this...this was more. She sighed as a finger skirted her clit, traced over her moist folds and lower to tease the awakening nerve endings of her puckered rosette. "Keep your eyes closed, babe."

He moved over her body, his erection prodding her entrance. Slowly, so slowly he pushed into her, the first magical stroke stretching her swollen tissues and sending even more anticipation rippling through her.

Fully embedded in her, he stilled to kiss her breasts. Nipping. Teasing. Sucking and soothing. Taking so much care she decided no other man would ever stand the comparison. He kissed her, stealing her breath and replacing it with his, implanting his will on her body and pushing her to scale heights she'd never imagined conquering.

Lana quivered and trembled, her pussy clutching his shaft. Pleasure radiated from her clit, streaking along her legs in languorous waves. Never before had it been like this. Never. Her breathing became choppy and her pulse rate raced. His touch soothed her, relaxing and taking her back to her serene bubble.

Finally, he moved, retreating and thrusting in measured strokes, each one a purposeful drag across her swollen nub. Her pulse rate ratcheted up again and the waves of pleasure came faster, more intense. When this happened, Duncan halted, and waited for her to calm. He kissed her, tugging her bottom lip into his mouth and soothing it with a glide of his tongue. He explored the interior, the contrasting hardness of her teeth and softness of her inner cheek before thrusting his tongue in and out of her mouth in imitation of the sexual act. Her breasts ached and her channel pulsed. A pained gasp escaped. Twice more he pushed her hard, building the sexual tension, stoking the fire burning inside her before easing her back to a low simmer.

"This time, babe. I want you to come for me. I want you to squeeze my cock tight and take me with you. That's it. Squeeze those inner muscles. Yeah." Duncan stroked in and out, increasing the pace of his thrusts.

She burned. Pleasure glowed through her body. Duncan hit her clit with his next thrust and she exploded, the sensations immense, powerful, shooting down her legs and up her body, surfing across her belly and breasts. The pleasure continued in sharp contractions. Duncan slammed into her hard, pushing her up the bed a fraction until the ropes around her ankles stopped the movement. He groaned, his big body trembling, his thrusts rapid and quick-fire. Then he stilled, and she thrilled at his dark groan of fulfillment.

She opened her eyes to find him looking at her. A blush suffused her face on seeing his expression. "That was amazing."

"More where that came from."

Lana wasn't sure her body could deal with more than what she'd just experienced, too sated to argue the point. Her eyes fluttered closed again. Duncan pulled from her body. He untied her arms and rubbed her shoulders for her before releasing her legs. He disappeared for a few seconds, the distant clank of pipes telling her he'd gone to the bathroom. When he appeared back in the bedroom, she'd hardly moved.

"Are you okay?" he asked, his voice tinged with concern.

"If I were any better, I'd turn into a puddle."

"I'll take that as a yes." His tone told her he was grinning, although she didn't open her eyes to confirm, not even when he cleaned her with a warm cloth. Sleep beckoned, besides, she didn't think she could move.

Duncan studied her, his heart beating faster than normal. That had been the most intense sexual experience he'd ever had. Lana was all and more than he'd expected. No way in hell he'd let her walk away, or worse, let another man snap her up again. Lana belonged to him, his woman, even if she hadn't admitted it yet, and it made him more determined to emerge the victor in this cat-and-mouse game.

Lana stood at the kitchen doorway and scanned her busy restaurant. Business had been slow the first couple of days after reopening, although once word traveled, the regulars returned and booked out most lunch and dinner sittings. Now in the second week after reopening, Lana had started to breathe easy again.

Her stomach roiled, and she swiped her hand over her forehead. Somehow she thought the flu might have caught up with her, despite telling her chef and waitresses she was all right.

Perhaps she'd go to her flat and rest now that the initial rush had died.

Suzy, one of her two waitresses took one look and said, "Flu. You've got it. Admit it and go up to bed before you vomit over a customer. Your face has turned green."

"Thanks for the compliment," Lana said.

"Garry, tell her," Suzy said, appealing to the chef.

"Go up to bed, boss. You don't want to spread the flu to us, do you?"

"Good argument," Suzy said.

Lana offered a weak smile and left them to run her restaurant. She rubbed her chest, attempting to push away the tight sensation. From experience she knew she'd bounce back quickly. Felines always did on the few occasions they succumbed to human illness. "I'm sure I'll feel better by tonight."

"We can cope," Gary said. "We might be stretched without you, but we'll limit the menu for tonight and deal with the rush. Tomorrow is Sunday and we're closed, so why don't you come back to work on Monday?" His expression said he doubted she'd be better by then. Lana nodded and trudged toward the back stairs that led to her apartment. When she reached the top stair, she fumbled with the doorknob and made a run for the bathroom. She just made it, vomiting into the toilet.

Five minutes later Lana traipsed to her bedroom and dropped onto the bed, her head aching now that she'd given in to the illness. She'd scarcely drawn breath when the urge to vomit claimed her again. The violent vomiting lasted throughout the night until she fell into a fitful sleep in the early hours of the morning. Her staff was right. The flu bug had caught her too.

Duncan thought of Lana often and rang twice during the week to hear her voice and discuss their separate days. It was difficult, giving her space, keeping their relationship on a casual level when all he wanted was to capture and lock her in his bedroom.

The restaurant didn't open on Sunday. Duncan picked up the phone and dialed her number. By the time six rings passed, a frown had built. Wasn't she home? The answer phone picked up the call, and he hesitated, not wanting to leave a message. Messages were easy to ignore. About to hang up, he heard Lana's voice over the welcoming message on the answer phone.

"Lana, it's Duncan. Are you okay?"

"Apart from throwing up all night. Yeah, I'm fine."

"You've got the flu?"

"Don't sound so surprised. It's been bad in the town."

"You're feline."

"Yeah." Lana snorted. "Proof that a feline can catch human diseases."

"I'll drop in and see you when I come to town."

"No, it's unnecessary. I'm not going anywhere. I'm so tired I'll spend most of the day dozing."

"Humor me. I won't stay for long, just check on you." After not seeing her for a week, there was no way he wouldn't drop by her place. A man could take only so much.

"All right." She capitulated with a loud yawn. "Ring the bell when you arrive."

"Take care." Duncan hung up before he said something to louse up his plan.

The phone jangled straightaway. Duncan picked it up with a smile on his face. "Did you forget something?"

"Duncan, I haven't forgotten a thing. I can't wait to see you again." Not Lana. Jennifer. Damn, the woman wouldn't leave him alone. He had his own stalker.

"You've caught me at a bad time, Jennifer. I'm on my way out." And he'd damn well think harder about getting caller identification installed on his phone or perhaps he'd change number and have the new one unlisted.

"I want to visit you."

"Can't talk, Jennifer. I've got to go." He hung up, grabbed his wallet and vehicle keys, ignoring the summons when the phone rang again.

One week later

The first person Lana thought of when she received an invitation to the swanky party was Duncan. Unfortunately, she couldn't commit career suicide and turn down the invitation.

Maybe she could ask Duncan to come along and make it more fun. Their hostess had a reputation for innovative cocktail snacks while the host took pride in his wine-buff status. There would be none of the cheap stuff at this party. As her thoughts centered on Duncan, a surge of lust speared her lower body. Okay, that did it. She'd proposition the man again. That had worked well last time, despite her concerns.

"A party?" Duncan asked when she rang. "You'd better help me pick out something to wear. I don't want to embarrass you."

Lana thought about that for two seconds. "I doubt you'd ever embarrass me. Okay. Bring your black trousers. They look good on you. We'll get a new shirt." She'd love to help choose his clothes. Studying his muscular body rated as a pleasure and never a hardship.

The days to the party passed slowly. Lana didn't think she'd been this excited about anything for ages, or maybe it was seeing Duncan again. He'd dropped by to check on her when she'd been sick and ended up spending the night. The next morning the illness had receded, and they'd even made love before he returned to his farm. That had been last week and seemed so long ago.

When Saturday arrived, Lana enjoyed shopping with Duncan. Her only regret was that they didn't have time to make love before they headed out to the party in one of the wealthy suburbs of Queenstown.

Lana knew a fair percentage of the attendees and took pleasure in introducing Duncan. It was easier and more fun attending with an escort rather than becoming the victim of a matchmaker hostess.

"I'm pleased to meet you, Duncan. I must find you later for a chat," Judith, their hostess, said. "She's kept silent about you."

"We're friends," Lana protested, frowning at Duncan's wince. The expressions flickered over his face so quickly she wondered if she'd been mistaken.

"They're cousins," Richard said, coming up behind Lana and sliding an arm around her waist.

Duncan's eyes narrowed with irritation. "The term is kissing cousins," he said, tugging Lana away from Richard's grasp and pulling her to his side.

Judith's brows rose and a smile of amusement followed. "I see."

Lana saw all too well but didn't intend to make an issue of Duncan's statement within Richard's hearing. Although she'd initially liked the lawyer and had accepted his requests for several dates, his possessive manner continued to annoy her.

"There are waiters circulating with food and drink. Help yourself, and, Lana, you know most of the people here. Introduce Duncan around and have fun," Judith said.

"You never said you were bringing someone," Richard said, his voice accusing.

"I didn't think it was any of your business. I'm going to introduce Duncan to everyone. See you later. Come on. You have to see the view over Lake Wakatipu and the night lights from the verandah. It's stunning." And hopefully it'd be quiet enough out there for a kiss or two. Lana took Duncan's hand and tugged him toward the sounds of music and chatter, the clink of glassware and laughter.

"Drink, madam? Sir?" The young waiter, dressed in black and white, stood while they made their selection from his tray.

With glasses in hand, they wove through the crowd, stopping here and there for Lana to make introductions.

Duncan played the perfect gentleman, fitting in so well she beamed. Jamie had hated this sort of thing, and after the first two occasions had refused to attend any others.

"What do you do, Duncan?" Judith's sister asked.

The usual getting-to-know-you and weighing questions to work out where Duncan came on the social scale. Lana sighed. This part she hated.

"I have my own farm," Duncan said.

"Oh? Whereabouts?" The sister sidled closer to Duncan and Lana ground her teeth in annoyance.

"Not far from Cromwell."

"A man of few words. I love me the strong, silent, handsome type." The sister trailed her hand over Duncan's chest, the long gray-tipped fingernails looking like claws. Personally, Lana preferred her natural feline claws, except she didn't think a show-and-tell would go well at the swanky cocktail party.

"Mine," Lana said.

"Oh." Judith's sister smirked. "I thought you were the consummate businesswoman with no intentions of remarrying. I'm sure Judith told me that at some stage. Do I have it wrong?"

"No," Lana said.

"Yes," Duncan said at the same time.

The woman's lips twitched. "I'm not sure I understand. Which is it?"

"We're good friends," Lana blurted before Duncan could reply.

"I see."

They needed to get away from the infuriating woman. "I see Maria and her husband. I wanted to introduce Duncan to them," Lana said, tugging on Duncan's forearm.

"It's nice to meet you. We'll chat later," the woman said.

Not if Lana had anything to do with it. She cast a quick glance at Duncan, worried what she might see. The last thing she wanted was for him to get ideas of them as a couple. She liked things the way they were. Oh heck. Just as she thought. His expression bore distinct satisfaction and the faint stamp of possessive ownership.

Lana led him over to Maria. After introductions and chitchat, they moved on, drifting toward the large balcony. A sigh of relief emerged once they stepped outside. The subtle and unsubtle questions regarding Duncan were getting on her nerves, putting her on edge. They weren't a couple. They were friends. A difference. She snorted. One her friends and business acquaintances couldn't seem to distinguish.

"Million-dollar view," Duncan said, walking over to the railing and staring out over the inky blackness of the lake.

"Yes." Lana loved the twinkling lights of the town. "See the lights of the gondola traveling up the hill?"

"Yeah."

"Is something wrong?"

"Of course not."

"Don't take any notice of the gossip. These people thrive on it."

This time Duncan snorted. "And you think the rodeo circuit is any better? It's a constant round of who is sleeping with whom and the latest romantic bust-up."

A cloud of jealousy fogged her mind at the thought and she gripped the railing in front of them. Damn, she didn't want to think of Duncan with other women. "I suppose there's gossip everywhere."

"Started with the cavemen," he said. "I don't want to discuss that. I'd much rather take advantage of the setting and the time with you." Taking her hand, he tugged her over to a dark corner occupied only by a fragrant lemon tree in a blue tub. He drew her against his chest and cupped her face between his hands, lowering his lips to cover hers. He stole her breath and yanked at her heart with the kiss, giving and taking at the same time. Lana groaned, sinking into his embrace and drawing his masculine scent deep to last her for the rest of the week. Although she'd never admit it, she'd missed him, and even worse, since he'd burst into her life, she'd craved sex. Even now her pussy moistened, preparing for his possession and the sweet way he mastered her. She quivered, her pulse ticking in a racy beat, senses full of his scent and taste.

By the time Duncan pulled away, her breath came in quick pants. She didn't even try to hide her arousal, merely stared up at him, craving more of his touch and recalled the sensual place he'd taken her when she'd visited his farm. Need bubbled through her and she wished they weren't in the middle of a party.

Duncan pushed her away from him. "Will you be okay on your own for a while?"

"Sure, I should say hello to a few more people."

"Good." He pressed a swift kiss to her lips before walking away.

Bemused, she wandered inside, wondering where he was going. She saw him speak to Judith and disappear.

"Ah, there you are, Lana."

Richard. Again. "I wanted to apologize for my behavior," he said, surprising her. "I haven't behaved well, heck, I've been rude, and I'm sorry. My only excuse is that I want more than friendship, and I'm afraid when I saw you with another man jealousy got the better of me. Will you accept my apology?"

"Of course I will." An apology wasn't something she'd expected.

"I'm glad you've found someone who makes you happy." Richard smiled, and it chopped ten years off his age, making his brown eyes sparkle. "If the way the man looks at you means what I think it does, it won't be long before we hear wedding bells."

"No, I don't think so." Duncan...it wasn't like that between them. Neither of them wanted serious or anything more than friendship. "We're just friends."

Richard nodded, except she saw he didn't believe a word of her denial. Duncan returned, appearing silently at her side.

"How is the farm going?" Richard asked.

Stunned by the lawyer's assertion, Lana studied Duncan with new eyes. Nah, Richard was wrong. Duncan didn't want a wife. He'd said so, hadn't he?

"Lana?"

Her head jerked up. "Did you say something?"

Richard laughed and moved away, leaving her alone with Duncan.

"What?" Lana asked when Duncan smirked.

"Nothing." He took her hand. "Come with me."

"Where are we going? We can't leave yet."

"We're not leaving," Duncan promised.

Mystified, she followed him from the crowded lounge, past a kitchen with a busy caterer and along a wide, carpeted passage. At the end of the passage, he turned right, and after a quick glance in both directions, he opened a door and urged her inside.

"This is a storage cupboard," she said when he stepped in with her and pulled the door shut, leaving them in inky darkness.

"Yeah." A rasp of a zipper sounded followed by the rustle of clothing. "Take off your panties."

Sudden excitement pounded through her veins as he lifted her black skirt and helped her skim her silky panties down her thighs. He kissed her again like he had out on the balcony, and need zapped the length of her body. His breath caressed her face while his hand skimmed her bare bottom.

"Unfasten your blouse and pull up your bra so I can touch your breasts."

Lana never considered disobeying. With shaky hands she slipped several buttons free of their holes and tugged at her lace bra, baring her breasts. Now that her eyes had adjusted to the dark, she saw the gleam of his before he lowered his head and sucked a nipple deep into his mouth. She moaned, when he slipped a finger into her pussy, gently stretching and testing her readiness.

"Got to get inside you," he muttered. "Now." He dragged his finger from her channel, skimming it over her clit before guiding his cock into her. "Curl your legs around me. I'll do the work."

Writhing in his grip and panting hard at the sheer naughtiness and with need, the sensual tension inside the dark cupboard increased. He pushed into her, gripping her hips while he shafted her deeply. There was nothing practiced or calm about this joining. Frantic, he grasped her hips and drove into her again and again, grunting with each hard thrust.

Lana hung on, thrilling to the masterful exhibition of his strength. He crushed her mouth under his and removed one hand to pinch her nipple. A ribbon of pain curled down to her pussy, combining with the hard stroke across her clit. The perfect touch to throw her into a maelstrom of pleasure. Her sex pulsed in hard spasms of pleasure and after one more powerful thrust, Duncan groaned in climax. Breathing hard, he held her against him while they both recovered from the experience.

"Lana, you're so hot," he said before claiming her mouth. When the kiss ended, he lifted her off his cock. "I have a hanky somewhere. My mother said I should never leave home without one in my pocket. No idea why since I rarely use it," he added with a laugh. "Here. You might need that to clean up."

With her heart still racing, Lana accepted the hanky and righted her clothes. The rustle of fabric indicated Duncan did the same. "Where are my panties?"

"They're in my pocket. Do you want them?" Voices outside the door made her freeze in horror.

"Come on, we could do it in here. Don't make me wait until we get home. I'm desperate for you," a man said, his husky voice full of persuasion.

"What if we get caught?" his feminine companion asked in clear doubt.

"We won't."

Lana squeezed closer to Duncan, horror filling her. They were going to get caught. Heat filled her cheeks along with panic.

"All right," the woman said.

Carpet muted their footsteps. The jangle of the doorknob sounded loud in the confines of the cupboard. Lana barely restrained her gasp.

"Damn, it's locked," the man said. "We'll have to find somewhere else."

Lana leaned into Duncan in sheer relief then the man's words registered. "Are we locked in here?"

"No, I had hold of the doorknob. We're good." He soothed her with a languid kiss and Lana let her fear drift away. This was the best business-related party she'd ever attended.

Chapter 9

Huge Shock

L ana stared at the pregnancy test in horror. Although pleased she could take the normal human test rather than making a special trip to Middlemarch to see the vet who doubled as a feline doctor, she hated the result.

Positive.

The familiar nauseous sensation in her stomach that had driven her to take the test in the first place made itself known. She swallowed to no avail, tossed the test aside and made a run for the bathroom, barely making it in time. Pregnant. The truth rippled through her mind, echoing endlessly. What the hell was she going to do?

Lana padded out to the passage, grabbed a flannel from the cupboard and returned to the bathroom. Soaking it with cool water, she wiped her face on autopilot.

Pregnant.

Trapped.

She'd have to tell Duncan. Lying didn't sit well. Besides, he'd guess her predicament soon. The other alternative...no...unthinkable. She'd have this child, the problem being the second she informed Duncan he'd order her to marry him. She'd be trapped just as she'd been with Jamie—a steel-tight trap since, with a child involved, Duncan would be motivated to get his way.

A wife and child in one swoop.

Yes, there was only one way he'd react. Excitement followed by mating—the possessive feline when a woman bore his child. He'd expect to raise his son or daughter, and if she refused, the rest of the feline community might shun her.

Her eyes stung, the lump in her throat testament to her anxiety.

What the hell was she going to do?

The phone rang.

"Lana, you ready to rock-and-roll here in the kitchen."

"Sorry, I slept in. I'll be there in a few minutes."

"Good-oh." The phone clunked when her chef hung up.

Lana sucked in a deep breath, deciding to cope with the present instead of the future. If this morning sickness continued to plan, she should be okay working in the kitchen.

Lana stripped off her sleep shirt and avoided a glance in the mirror. Pregnancy and its reality didn't appeal now or in the future. She jumped under the shower. Ten minutes later she entered the kitchen determined to concentrate on business instead of Duncan and the baby.

The next couple of days continued in the same vein. Sick as soon as she woke. After a shower and a piece of dry toast her stomach settled enough to work. Thankfully Duncan had gone on a trip to Christchurch to attend a cattle sale. He'd rung her and she'd let the answer phone pick up his calls.

On the third night she sat in her dark apartment, trying to work out what to do. She needed to visit the doctor in Middlemarch. Picking up the phone, she rang Gavin and made an appointment for the following evening.

"Lana! How nice to see you." Emily bustled around the counter of her café and hugged her. "What are you doing here?"

Fresh from her doctor's appointment, tears welled into her eyes and splashed her cheeks.

With a concerned look, Emily hustled her out the back to her kitchen. "Here. Sit." She pushed a stool toward Lana. "What's wrong?"

"I'm pregnant," Lana blurted, every bit of fear and panic she was experiencing echoing in the two words.

"Oh Lana." Emily's arms came around her in a warm hug. "Is it Duncan's baby?"

"Yes," Lana sobbed.

"And you haven't told him."

Lana accepted the hanky Emily produced and tried not to think about the way Duncan always carried a handkerchief in his pocket because his mother had told him to. "No, I haven't seen him this week."

"I don't think you need to worry, Lana. Duncan will be ecstatic. He'll want to mate with you."

Lana mopped her tears with the white hanky. "That's the problem. Jamie loved me. I know he did, but he hated me working. He wanted me to stay at home and I couldn't do that. Toward the end, our arguments were so bitter. If he hadn't died, I think we might have parted by now. He didn't know I took the Pill to prevent pregnancy."

"Oh," Emily said. "You can't not tell Duncan. Felines love children..." she trailed off, and they stared at each other in pained silence.

"Jamie thought I couldn't get pregnant because I always rushed around at work and didn't relax enough."

Emily snorted. "I take it sex wasn't a problem."

"No. It's a problem this time," she said glumly. "I should have remained celibate and then this wouldn't be happening. It's just that I hadn't had sex for so long and I craved a man's touch."

"I understand that. You know I was married to a human before Saber?" At Lana's nod, she continued. "He cheated on me. I hadn't had sex for months and came to attend the Middlemarch ball because I wanted to have fun and get laid."

"What happened?" Lana asked.

"I met Saber, and we had sex. I missed the train back to Dunedin and stayed with Saber. The man convinced me we were meant for each other and I'm still here."

"Are you trying to have children?"

"Not yet," Emily said, unperturbed by the personal question. "Saber said he wanted me to himself for a while and that it wouldn't hurt to practice, but we've discussed it again recently." She shook her head and grinned. "We'll see. The man sure does like to practice. You know Duncan and Saber are alike. I'm sure if you talked to Duncan you could work something out."

Lana sighed. "I know I need to talk to him." She hesitated and swallowed. "I'm frightened. I can't see any alternatives."

"Do you love Duncan?"

"I've tried not to think about it. All I wanted was a weekend of good sex. I didn't even mean to see him again."

"But you have," Emily said, a twinkle in her eyes. "Doesn't that tell you something?"

"That feline men are persuasive."

The front door of the restaurant opened and firm footsteps sounded. Saber strode into the kitchen, coming to an abrupt halt.

He frowned at Lana's tearstained face. "Everything okay?"

"We're fine," Emily said. "You'll stay the night, Lana? Sly and Joe are at home and you've met them before. They'll enjoy the feminine company."

"But—"

"You can see Duncan tomorrow," Emily said.

Early the next morning, Emily waved Lana off with parting advice.

"Tell the truth, everything, including your fears." According to Emily, they couldn't fix potential problems between them if they weren't honest with each other from the outset.

"Okay." The reply came automatically to reassure herself as much as Emily. Fear stalked her mind already at the thought of confronting Duncan. He was feline male and Jamie's cousin. Like the rest of the feline males, he possessed instincts to protect and nurture. He'd want to offer security, which for a feline meant mating.

Trapped.

Lana suppressed a shudder and started her car, backing from the driveway. With a last farewell wave at Emily, she drove toward the township and her visit to Duncan. No matter how Emily spun this pregnancy as positive, Lana couldn't help seeing disaster ahead.

The morning sickness hit around the usual time. Lana pulled over on the side of the road and vomited on the dry grass verge. Breathing deep, she waited out the worst of the sickness before rummaging in her bag for the dry crackers Emily had given her after she'd refused breakfast. Fifteen minutes later, stomach settled, she continued her journey. The miles ticked over and her nerves increased until her stomach lurched with sickness again.

Trapped.

Tears stung her eyes and one escaped, rolling down her cheek. Her hands clutched the steering wheel with a white-knuckle grip. Lana swallowed and indicated left, pulling onto the road where Duncan lived. Unable to ring because in her fragile state she thought she'd start blubbering, she'd arrived early and hoped she'd catch him before he started his chores for the day. A breath eased out in relief when she saw his SUV parked outside his house. A second SUV, one she didn't recognize, had parked beside it. She pulled up and switched off the ignition, inhaling twice, hoping to settle her nerves. With trembling legs, she climbed out of the car.

"Lana!" Duncan's smile was broad and welcoming. "Why didn't you tell me you were coming?" He strode toward her, arms outstretched, and grabbed her in a hug before pulling back to kiss her.

Some of the panic inside eased at his touch and obvious pleasure in seeing her. Since learning of her pregnancy, she worried how he'd react. Now the fear started to grow about how to tell him. She didn't want to blurt it out.

"Have I come at a bad time? You have visitors," she said.

"Lana, you're welcome to visit any time you want. Come inside so I can say hello properly." His eyes gleamed and amusement washed through her at his obvious thoughts.

"You have visitors."

"Leaving," he said, his tone curt. "I tried to ring you yesterday and last night. Ended up leaving messages."

"I've been busy." Lana walked at his side, the weight of his arm around her shoulders soothing her agitation.

"How long can you stay? I have a load of cattle arriving in an hour."

A small squeak and a blur of movement attracted Lana's attention. A half-naked Jennifer stood in the kitchen, her arms crossed over her bare breasts. "Oh, I didn't know you were bringing your visitor inside," she said.

A streak of pain stabbed Lana straight through the heart, and in that moment she knew this thing with Duncan was more than friendship. She cared enough that he could hurt her, had hurt her. She glanced past the counter and her gaze settled on a flimsy royal blue robe draped over a chair. It didn't belong to her. "I'm in the way. I'll go."

"No, Lana." Duncan grasped her arm and halted her retreat. "This isn't what it looks like. Jennifer, what the hell are you doing? Get dressed."

The woman pouted and dropped her arms to her sides to grab the robe. "Duncan, I'm sorry. I didn't expect you to bring anyone into the kitchen." After belting the robe at her waist she turned to Lana. "Would you like a cup of tea?"

Lana's mouth dropped open in shock before swirling chagrin and anger formed a solid ball in the pit of her stomach. She wrenched from Duncan's grip and backed toward the door.

"Jennifer," Duncan snapped.

"She should go," Jennifer said. "She's spoiling my announcement. I wanted to be alone, but I might as well just tell you. I'm pregnant! You're going to be a daddy."

Lana turned and fled. Shock held her together while she started her car and whipped down Duncan's driveway. In her rear-vision mirror she saw Duncan run out of the house. Seconds later Jennifer joined him, cuddling up to him like a sex kitten. The honk of a horn dragged her back to the present, and she slowed, pulling over to allow a stock truck to pass on the narrow road. With one last anguished glance at the couple standing in front of the house, she concentrated on her driving so she made it back to Queenstown without having an accident. A baby counted on her. For five minutes she held it together before the tears flowed. Her vision blurred, her chest ached. Lana pulled off the road and gave in to the tears, screwing up her face and chest heaving with the strength of her sobs.

The scene flashed before her eyes. Duncan and Jennifer. She'd seen them together several times and never guessed. Her entire body stiffened, agony flooding mind and limbs. The idea of Jennifer laughing behind her back...it shouldn't have mattered. It did. Had he been seeing Jennifer all this time while he'd been sleeping with her? She clamped her eyes shut, curling her body over the steering wheel, a whimper squeezing past the lump in her throat.

The ironic thing—one that crystallized in her mind—she'd fallen for Duncan harder than she'd either wanted or suspected and it was too late. She couldn't have him.

"What the fuck are you talking about?" Duncan snarled at Jennifer. He pushed her away from him and she returned like a magnet, her hands reaching in an attempt to cling. "I haven't slept with you since the bull ride carnival in South Auckland. Six months ago." He removed her hands again and stepped out of range, restricting himself to glaring when he wanted to wring her neck so badly his hands shook. "I've told you. I'm seeing someone else and I'm not interested in you."

"You will sleep with me," Jennifer said, flashing him a brilliant smile while thrusting out her chest enough to make her robe gape. Her air of self-confidence grated and made him want to lash out.

"No, I'm not." The need to wring her neck increased, and he spat out a pithy curse. The creamy curves did nothing for him, not when he ached for Lana. God, her expression… He brushed past Jennifer, heading inside to grab his keys. Lana would listen to him. She had to.

Almost inside, the approach of a vehicle grabbed his attention. Damn, the cattle truck. He wouldn't be going anywhere for a few hours.

"I'm going to unload the cattle. Make sure you're gone by the time I get back."

"I love you," Jennifer said.

"Bullshit," Duncan spat. "One last time. I don't want you. I'm not interested."

"What about your reputation? How do you think people will react when they learn I'm pregnant and you're refusing to take responsibility?"

"I don't give a fuck," Duncan said, and he spoke the truth.

"I'll tell everyone."

"Do your worst." Duncan didn't think things could get worse. Lana thought he'd lied to her, that he'd slept with Jennifer and made her pregnant. He turned and walked away without looking back.

Duncan walked into the restaurant shortly before closing time. Good. With only one table still occupied, Lana couldn't pretend she didn't have time to talk to him. He knew the second she spotted him. Her body tensed and the stack of dirty dishes she held went flying. They crashed to the tiled floor, attracting the attention of the remaining customers and her staff.

"Are you okay?" Duncan hated the signs of distress on her face, hated knowing he'd caused so much anguish.

"Go away," she said in a strained voice. "I don't want to talk to you." She pushed through a set of double doors and returned straightaway with a broom and dustpan.

"Let me help." Duncan stooped to pick up several of the larger pieces of china.

"There is nothing between us. Please just go away and leave me alone." Her words were thick with tears.

"Do you need a hand, Lana?" a young male waiter asked.

"Yeah, I'm clumsy." Lana swept up the shards of china and scraps of food.

"Please, all I want is a chance to talk. Ten minutes, and after that if you still want me to leave, I will."

Lana refused to meet his gaze and gave a jerky nod instead. "Wait for me upstairs."

A good decision because he didn't intend to leave until they'd talked. He studied her bent head for a little longer before standing. Duncan left because he thought she'd prefer to have their discussion away from customers and staff.

Up in her apartment, he prowled from room to room, pausing to pick up a magazine only to toss it aside. His ears strained to hear what was happening in the restaurant. The murmur of voices. The slam of a door. He circled the room again, wondering how he could make Lana believe him. He should come clean and tell her how much he loved her. Something twisted in his chest, a sense of bitterness and raw, primitive grief. He'd missed out on his chance with Lana before because he'd stood aside for Jamie.

He couldn't—wouldn't—do it again.

God, if only she believed him. He wanted, craved her so much. When they weren't together, he thought about her. They were meant for each other. He didn't want Jennifer and hadn't looked at another woman since hooking up with Lana at the rodeo in Middlemarch.

Halfway through another restless circuit of the room, he heard the creak of the stairs. Lana appeared seconds later, her expression guarded and her body drooping with exhaustion. An ache stirred in the region of his heart and he wanted to go to her, but she raised her hands as if to ward him off.

"No, don't touch me," she said, reinforcing her body language. "Tell me what you have to and leave. I'm tired and I want to go to bed."

"Would you like me to make you a cup of tea?" Duncan made the offer, expecting her to reject his suggestion.

"Thank you. A cup of chamomile tea might help me sleep."

Nodding, Duncan walked over to the kitchen and plugged in the jug. Surprised she'd accepted his offer, he went through the motions of making the tea while observing Lana. Exhaustion weighed down her slender body, her shoulders slumped into the brown couch. He noted the purple shadows beneath her closed eyes and the pale face. Her clear vulnerability tore at his heart. The urge to close the distance between them and gather her into his arms almost got the better of him. He had to force himself to remain where he stood, hating the inactivity because he always fixed things. Something told him this wouldn't be quite as easy.

When the water boiled, he poured it over the tea bag, dunking it several times in the mug before discarding it. Under normal circumstances she'd chide him for not letting the tea steep long enough. Tonight he wondered if she'd even notice.

"Here you go." He handed the mug over, frowning at the tremor of her hands and the way she refused to meet his gaze. "Are you sure you're okay?"

"Yes." Her voice cracked, and the tremor spread to her lips. Duncan's scowl intensified when she tried to hide it by taking a sip of her tea. What the hell was going on with her? He'd never seen her like this before.

He waited for her to say more, expected it, except she seemed content to sip her tea. A deep inhalation did nothing to settle the disquiet flickering through him.

Bugger, Jennifer. He'd never encouraged her, although he'd slept with her twice. Obviously where he'd made his mistake—allowing his cock to rule good sense. Luckily he'd wised up.

"It's true I've slept with Jennifer before, not since we met again in Middlemarch though. I have done nothing except talk to her for the last six months." His mouth tightened at her clear disbelief. "I'm not a bloody monk. I like sex, so shoot me."

"Jennifer says she's pregnant. What are you going to do?"

"Didn't you hear me? If she's pregnant, it's not mine. I'm willing to take tests to prove it."

Lana glanced at him then, her face shrouded with pain, her beautiful eyes shiny with unshed tears. "I thought you'd be like every feline male—ecstatic at becoming a father."

Duncan's mouth dropped open in shock. The accusation, the pain and acres of hurt in her voice made him silently curse his cousin Jamie. Damn the man for messing with Lana's head.

It was obvious to him that Jamie had stuffed up big time, causing a few mental scars in his wife.

"Of course I want kids," he said, striving to give her honesty and wanting to ease her mind. "That doesn't mean I fuck indiscriminatingly, intending to populate the world with my feline offspring. I always use condoms." Usually. Except with Lana. "As for Jennifer, I'm not about to bring her into the feline world when it's obvious she's lying. Lies are no foundation for a relationship."

"You didn't use condoms with me."

"No." Shit, he could hardly tell her he'd wanted to get her pregnant, subconsciously at least.

A tear overflowed, swiftly followed by another. She squeezed her eyes shut. The tears didn't stop. Her chest rose in a sob, the sound escaping despite her effort to retain it.

To hell with this. Duncan moved swiftly, taking the tea from her hands and setting it aside. He sat beside her and hauled her against his chest. "I'm so sorry. I didn't mean to hurt you." He smoothed his hand over her back, relieved to have her close enough to touch and take into his arms.

For a long time she sobbed, and he held her, murmuring nonsense and stroking her back. Finally the tears stopped coming, and she quieted.

"Jamie wanted children. He wanted children before we married. I wanted to wait because of my restaurant. I loved him although toward the end things were bad. He wanted me to sell the restaurant and stay home. We argued the day of the accident."

"I knew it had to be something like that." Which was the reason he'd taken a cautious approach even though everything in him had chafed at the delay.

"Are you going to marry Jennifer?"

"For the last time, no. If she's pregnant, it's not my child. I don't love her and this stunt of hers has dropped her in my estimation. I'll be steering clear of the woman." Duncan meant every single word.

"Oh." Lana started crying again, and he reached the end of his patience.

"What the fuck is wrong? Spit it out and I'll fix it," he snapped, putting her away from him and standing.

"You can't fix it."

"Tell me."

"I'm pregnant," Lana said, glaring at him with belligerent eyes.

Shock rippled through Duncan and he dropped to the couch again, his knees suddenly too weak to hold his weight. "How?"

Lana gave him a mocking smile and didn't pull it off. "The usual way. I had the flu and forgot to take my pills."

"Who—"

Lana leapt to her feet. "The only man I've had sex with is you. I'm not like you. I don't sleep around. That makes you the father," she ended on a screech.

Shock turned to acceptance and acceptance to excitement. A baby with Lana. Hell, he couldn't have planned better. "Good. Marry me," he said.

Chapter 10

A Future

It was happening already—the feline genes exerting themselves in bossy orders. Next would come the demand she give up work and become a good housewife and mother.

"I don't want to discuss it. You know the truth now and can leave." Lana dragged her weary body over to the door and opened it, standing to the side while waiting for him to depart.

Duncan strode to her side and shut the door. "You're exhausted, so we'll talk later, but I'm not leaving you like this, thinking I'm going to walk away."

"I don't need you," Lana snapped.

"You can't do it on your own. Dammit, I'm not Jamie. He was my cousin, and I loved him. He had his faults and could be a stubborn son of a bitch. Come on. Let's go to bed." He took her arm and Lana found herself propelled toward the bedroom. She was too tired to fight him.

"You can sleep on the couch."

Duncan ignored her and unfastened the buttons of her blouse.

"I'm not having sex with you."

"What kind of man do you think I am? You're tired and almost falling on your face. Stop arguing and get in bed."

He helped her remove her clothes and pulled back the sheets for her to slide into bed. Physical exhaustion tugged at her and she drifted toward sleep. She was vaguely aware of the mattress depressing beside her and Duncan wrapping an arm around her waist. A protest formed and faded because fatigue claimed her. Too tired to fight.

Lana woke slowly, her eyes opening cautiously as they had since she'd started suffering from morning sickness. Then she realized she wasn't alone. A masculine body cuddled up to hers. Duncan. Memories of the previous evening rushed back to her. She'd told him everything.

"Lana. You're awake," he murmured, his fingers trailing up and down her bare arm.

She rolled away and her stomach lurched. Lana jumped from bed and sprinted for the bathroom, barely making it in time. When she felt well enough to leave, she found Duncan waiting for her.

"Can I get you something?"

"Dry crackers from the pantry." Lana watched him walk away, torn by conflicting emotions. Why was he still here? Oh yeah. He probably wanted to claim their child, which landed her in the same trouble yet again. He couldn't bulldoze her into mating. No way. No how. Although she had no idea how things would play out, anything would be better than repeating the mess with Jamie.

"Here you go. Do you want tea?"

"Not yet," she said. What was with all the domestic stuff? It didn't impress her much. She nibbled on the crackers.

"Have you visited a doctor?" His gaze dipped to linger on her stomach.

Realizing she wore not a stitch, Lana grabbed a wrap from behind the door and yanked it on to cover her body. "Yes. When are you leaving?"

"I'm not."

"There's nothing to discuss," Lana said, her tone snippy. She turned away and walked to the kitchen. Luckily the crackers had settled her stomach. All going well she might get to the restaurant earlier than usual.

Duncan padded up behind her, grasping her forearm and propelling her into the lounge. "This isn't settled."

Lana lifted her chin, her eyes narrowing. "Duncan, just leave. It's been nice, but it's over. We both knew it wouldn't last." She wrenched from his touch and walked across to the couch, sitting and nibbling on a cracker while pretending disinterest. Inside she cried at the situation she found herself in with Duncan.

"Bullshit," Duncan growled. "Dammit, woman. I love you. I've loved you for a long time and damned if I'm going to walk away. Did you hear me?" he roared. "I love you."

"I suspect they heard you in Middlemarch," she said after a long pause where they stared at each other. He loved her? The *oomph* faded from anger, her annoyance softening.

"Aren't you going to say something?"

"Like what? It changes nothing." And it didn't. The same problems remained.

Duncan cursed. "Bloody Jamie. If he were here, I'd smack him one." He prowled across the room and sat at her side, taking her hand in his. "I love you. That doesn't mean I expect you to follow my every order or give up your restaurant. We're adults. We can plan something that works for both of us." He traced his fingers over the back of her hands, bringing a shiver. "There's no reason we couldn't hire a housekeeper or nanny or combination of the two. If you can think of something else to make things easier, we'll do it. I refuse to walk away from you again."

"Again?"

"I've loved you for a long time, Lana, since before you mated with Jamie."

"You never said anything," she said, surprised.

"I'm saying it now. I love you, we will mate and that's final." His scowl dared her to disagree.

Lana melted inside. She wanted to say yes, but instinct long ingrained held her back.

"Do you love me?" he demanded.

"Yeah."

"Don't sound so happy."

A laugh escaped Lana and his glower dissolved into a grin. "What if we tried a compromise?"

"I'm listening."

"Could we live together for a while first?"

"You want to ease into it to make sure I keep my word," Duncan said. "Make sure I don't change and order you to stay home and have babies."

Said like that, it made her feel terrible. "Jamie changed."

Duncan laughed. "No need to get defensive. We can live together and take things slow. I'm fine with that as long as you'll consider mating." He caressed her cheek and traced his fingers across her lips. "I know what I want. I want you."

Something inside her cracked, emotions pouring through her both cleansing and empowering. Lana melted into his arms, realizing she'd been fighting something she wanted since the weekend of the rodeo. This might work after all. Their lips met, drifting together in a kiss of promise, of giving and taking and intimacy. When they pulled apart, his expression held open love, stealing her breath with the sweetness and sheer need.

Duncan cupped her cheek with his hand. "Walk into the future with me?"

"One day at a time, right?"

"Anyway you want, sweetheart. We'll make this work."

"Yes." Lana smiled and leaned over to kiss him again. Somehow, she thought they would make their relationship work.

Three Months Later

Lana prowled into the sunny room they used as an office. "Duncan, I need sex. *Now*."

"Isn't that what got you into trouble in the first place?" His green eyes twinkled, his gaze running over her so intimately it felt as if he glided his hand over her bare arm. Duncan liked to touch, to stroke.

The thought of his callused fingers trailing over her naked body brought a rash of chill bumps to her skin and the steady thrum of desire. She backed up two steps and unfastened the plain cotton blouse she wore, following that with her bra. Her clothes whispered to the ground and a soft groan escaped when her heavy breasts spilled free. With her pregnancy they were much bigger and more sensitive. Lana tugged the loose black skirt down her legs and stepped out of it, leaving herself naked.

Duncan leaned back in his chair, making it squeak a protest. Traces of a smile played on his mouth. "No panties?"

"I thought it might save time."

"It's getting colder," he observed, a possessive expression on his face when his eyes skimmed her swollen belly.

Lana took pleasure in his scrutiny, even if she didn't let it show. She was his, just as he belonged to her. It was time. "I'm not cold." No, inside she burned with desperate need. This pregnancy had done more than swell her belly and breasts. It had made her horny. "If you're just going to sit there, I'll do the job myself."

"I'm not sure what you have in mind. Spell it out for me."

She could do that. In fact, Lana knew the perfect way to spell it out for him. "You should take off your shirt," she said. "It's going to get hot in here."

His brows rose, and she caught a flash of teeth when he grinned. "I guess I could do that." Seconds later, his denim shirt hit the floor.

Lana skimmed her fingers across the plump curve of one breast and pinched a nipple. A ribbon of sensation sped straight to her clit, and she moaned, so good she repeated the move before widening her stance. This time her hand smoothed over her belly and slipped between her legs. She grazed her clit, taking the teasing a notch higher. Her folds were damp with her arousal and the buzz of pleasure told her it wouldn't take long to get off. She didn't want that.

"Is there a reason I needed to take off my shirt?"

"Yeah, to improve the scenery," she said, stroking herself again for the sheer pleasure of it.

"Maybe I should ring for Leo Mitchell. He's the pretty one according to the gossip I heard last time I visited the vineyard."

"Nah, I don't need Leo. Besides, Isabella might object." Leo might look fine, but it was Duncan she lusted after. Without dropping her gaze, she sauntered toward him, hips swaying. Unable to resist, she leaned over, rubbed her breasts against his chest and stole a kiss.

"Hmm, I don't need to finish this bookwork right now." His hands spanned her waist and in one easy move, he lifted her onto his lap, arranging her body so they faced each other. Her legs splayed, leaving her wide open.

"Good decision." Lana nuzzled his neck, nipping him before soothing the spot with a moist kiss.

"I love you," Duncan whispered.

His words gave her a thrill as they always did. "I love you too. Touch me."

"With pleasure." He cupped a breast and dipped his head, taking her nipple into his mouth. The hard draw of his mouth made her groan. The gentle massage of his hand on her other breast sent currents of enjoyment through her. Arching into him, she silently encouraged greater pressure.

"Duncan, more. I need more."

Duncan let her nipple go to grin at her. "Woman, you're wearing me out. I'm still recovering from this morning."

Lana snorted. "You got me in this situation, you deal with the consequences."

"Are you going to let me take off my jeans?"

"Not yet. I thought I'd get you as hot and needy as I am first."

He leaned back a fraction, still grinning at her. "Do your worst."

Lana couldn't restrain her own smile. If she did this right, she'd bet she wouldn't even need to walk to the bedroom. He'd go all alpha on her and stride down the passage to their bedroom carrying her. Even thinking about it, her feline exerted its will. Claws grew beneath her fingernails and her teeth began their change. A growl sounded. Her growl.

"I love you," Lana said, and she kissed his lips before striking at his neck. Her teeth bit through his flesh, his body bucking against hers. Instead of yanking away, his hand cupped her head, holding her close. He groaned, his entire body shuddering as her tongue rasped across the place she'd bitten him. With one final lap of her tongue, she released him. "Mine."

His eyes glowed an eerie green, his feline close to the surface. In a swift move, he stood, sweeping her into his arms. The trip to their bedroom passed in the blink of an eye and she scarcely had time to move before he'd stripped off his jeans, boxers and socks to join her on the bed.

"You've marked me."

"Yes." And she didn't regret it in the slightest. He'd proven time and again how much he loved her, cared for her. It was the little things like bringing her a cup of tea in bed, giving her a backrub and ringing to say hello in the middle of the day, even though she knew he'd been busy. The way he helped to wash her hair when she was so tired she could hardly stand but needed to rid her body of the cooking smells because they made her nauseous. Duncan wanted her and the baby.

"It hurt."

"Yes."

"On your hands and knees," he ordered.

Without argument Lana rolled and pushed up on hands and knees. A shudder of delight pulsed through her and she felt the wetness at her core. Whenever he issued orders in that tone her body softened and prepared for his possession. She enjoyed submitting to him in the bedroom.

"I don't want to hurt you."

"You won't," she said with utter confidence.

Duncan took his time. The skim of his hands sent a warming shiver from head to toe until each inch of her skin tingled. His breath warmed her inner thighs and the lash of his tongue across her clit made her eyes flutter closed. Spending the rest of her life with this feline male no longer filled her with panic. Instead love engulfed her with each sensual caress of his hands. Her heart pounded as he kissed her spine, whispering his love for her with each soft caress. Carefully, he widened her stance and moved behind her, guiding his cock to her.

Lana held her breath when he pushed into her, the slow stretching of her sensitive tissues feeling so good her breath hitched. He kept pushing into her until he was balls deep.

"Lana," he said, his voice breaking. "I love you so much." He pulled out and thrust into her again, curling over her spine. His lips brushed the flesh at the juncture of neck and shoulder and his teeth nibbled on the delicate skin.

"Do that again," she said.

"I'm in charge."

"Yes."

"You belong to me."

"Yes," Lana agreed. "And you belong to me."

"I do." Duncan licked back and forth across her skin until she trembled with desire. He surged and retreated, making love to her, allowing need to build. One of his fingers teased her clit, timing his strokes with his thrusts. The pleasure grew from a tiny pinpoint at her clit, enlarging until it cascaded over her entire length. She groaned, the pleasure so great it was almost painful. Then she shattered, a powerful explosion that made her gasp. Duncan surged into her with swift strokes until his cock jerked with explosive contractions. At the same time his sharp teeth sliced into the flesh at her neck, his tongue lapping away the bleeding.

They remained like that for long moments. Duncan finally moved, pulling from her body and drawing her into his arms.

"Mine," he said.

Lana kissed him and whispered yes, her heart full of love for this feline male.

"We belong to each other," he said with clear satisfaction, and started making love to her again.

Lana slid her lips against his, glorying in his kiss, the competent and possessive grip of his hands. No doubt about it, she belonged with Duncan, and there was no place she'd rather be.

Chapter 11

Bonus Chapter

Mitchell Farm, Middlemarch, New Zealand

Feline Shapeshifter Council Meeting.

Present: Saber Mitchell, Sid Blackburn, Kenneth Nesbitt, Agnes Paisley, Valerie McClintock, Benjamin Urquart

"This idea to allow suggestions from the community is turning into a farce." The tip of Valerie's narrow nose quivered and her nostrils flared. She reached into her handbag and pulled out a sheaf of papers. They thumped to the table, and Saber noticed the black surge of claws beneath her fingernails as the cups rattled on their fine china saucers.

Sid reached out and patted her hand. "It can't be that bad."

"It's worse," Agnes snapped. "I thought felines were clever and intelligent. I'm doubting my assessment."

Curious, Saber glanced at the assortment of papers—different colors, different pen inks, different handwriting. "May I?" he asked Valerie.

She gestured *have at it* and reached for a pikelet topped with strawberry jam and whipped cream.

"Read them out, lad," Sid said. "I'll write a list."

Agnes sniffed, her lips pursed in a disapproving prune. "Disregard the ones without names. They shouldn't be counted."

Saber picked up a pile and scanned the first. His brows rose.

"Read it," Valerie snapped.

Saber glanced at the men and received a nod from each. He shrugged. This was turning into an interesting meeting, and it wasn't his job to head off trouble. Not all the time.

"Wet T-shirt competition at the pub," he read aloud.

"See? See what I mean?" Valerie demanded.

Agnes sniffed. "Who suggested that? Is there a name?"

Saber glanced at the men and again they nodded. "Brian Paisley Junior."

Agnes hissed and bristled, the salt-and-pepper hair on her head lifting in a catlike manner.

"Your grandson?" Valerie asked. "I expected better from your family."

"Now, now. None of that," Sid said in his amiable manner. "Boys will be boys. Read the next lad."

"A rave," Saber said. "Edwina McClintock."

"What's a rave?" Kenneth asked.

191

"Is-is that a bad thing?" Valerie asked in a faint voice. "I can't believe my granddaughter would suggest something wicked."

Kenneth pulled out a fancy smartphone and tapped several keys. "A rave is to talk wildly or incoherently. It also means to speak about something with enthusiasm or admiration." He pulled out a hanky to mop his brow. "I don't understand."

"Why do they want a speech competition?" Ben wrinkled his pixie nose, his piercing green gaze stabbing at each of them and broadcasting confusion.

Saber swallowed his chuckle. "In modern terms a rave is an underground party with electronic music."

Agnes sniffed. "An excuse to have sex and take drugs."

"Not necessarily," Saber said. "I don't think a rave would work here in the country, but we could have a day-long music festival with a variety of acts."

"No," Agnes said.

Valerie took off her glasses and peered at the lenses. "Definitely not."

"I like country music," Kenneth said. "We could invite that Keith Urban bloke. He has New Zealand connections."

Saber fought a grin and shuffled the papers in his hand.

Sid scrawled in his notebook. "I've added it to the list. What's next, lad?"

"A treasure hunt," Saber said.

"A treasure hunt?" Kenneth asked. "For children?"

"No, they'll mean something like those reality shows," Ben said. "I bet that's what they mean."

"Who suggested it?" Valerie asked. "We can check with them as to what they have in mind."

"Jason Reagen." At this rate, they'd never finish. Saber moved on before their questions diverted the meeting again. "A progressive dinner."

Agnes nodded. "Good idea."

In the brief pause, Saber inserted the next suggestion. "A picnic sports day."

Nods all around for this idea. Saber rather liked it himself.

"Sheep dog trials. Speed dating. Beauty contest. Street party. Craft or hobby show."

"Some workable suggestions," Kenneth said. "Are we still doing the haunted house for Halloween?"

"I think it will work well," Ben said. "You know I read of a town in America doing a cemetery tour. There is no reason we couldn't do one for the feline section. It could tie in with the haunted house for Halloween. There is a lot of history and the older felines have wonderful stories of when the leap first arrived in New Zealand and the journey over on the ships. Felines only, of course, but that might stir interest in our roots. I think roots are important."

Valerie reached for her tea and took a sip. "As long as we can keep it feline only."

"It occurs to me we could make it a mixed tour since the non-feline graves have interesting tales too. Halloween would be perfect because the non-feline people will think we're cashing in on the black cat sightings and making things up." Saber winked

193

at Sid. "We could always stage another one-off sighting to drum up interest."

"Never!" Agnes snapped.

Ben chuckled. "He's joking. Aren't you?"

Saber's grin widened, rather enjoying teasing them. "Something to consider. Next idea is a big garage sale or a flea market."

"One man's junk is another's riches," Kenneth quipped.

"Christmas caroling. Easter egg hunt. We've missed Easter for this year, but that's something we should do next Easter," Saber said.

"We could do a Christmas in the Park event and hold it at the school. On the rugby field if it's fine or in the hall," Kenneth said. "Combine it with a picnic dinner or lunch. I like that idea."

"A trivia night," Saber set aside the last paper in his hand and reached for more. "Wet T-shirt contest. A clown entertainer. Face painting. Drawing contest. Sevens rugby tournament. Kissing booth, gala day, a movie night, school camp, book club, disco party, afternoon tea, town mural, wet T-shirt contest, talent quest, wet T-shirt contest."

"The T-shirt is a popular idea." Ben kept his voice mild, but his eyes sparked with humor.

"I don't care how popular it is," Valerie snapped. "It's undignified."

"No one is saying a female has to wear the T-shirt," Saber said. "We asked for suggestions and our community has given them. We should study each on its merits."

"Lad is right," Sid said. "We've received several excellent ideas so far. I think we should consider each one. What's next, lad?"

Saber read more suggestions. "Casino night, speed dating, obstacle course, wet T-shirt contest, a dare contest."

"What's that?" Ben asked.

"I'll check on my phone." Kenneth hit buttons. "Ah, people make dares such as singing in public, dressing in a costume, shaving off a beard or coloring hair. People pay a dollar amount and then the people they dare have to carry out the dare."

Valerie let out an unladylike snort. "What happens if it's a stupid dare or an illegal one?"

"You can set the dares. I like the idea of making people sing in public. It would be an impromptu concert all week on the main street," Kenneth said. "I think we should do this one. I dare you Agnes. You sing like a bull frog."

"I have a good singing voice," Agnes said, lifting her nose into the air.

"If you're a lady frog searching for a mate," Ben said.

"I'll add it to the list," Sid said hastily. "Any more, lad?"

"Design a Middlemarch T-shirt contest, bingo night, used book sale, wet T-shirt contest, scavenger hunt, car wash, duck race on the river, community recipe book, triathlon, wet T-shirt contest, cooking school, cooking classes for men, cooking classes for kids, massage parlor, wet T-shirt contest, sports day, break a world record, wet T-shirt contest. That's it," Saber said.

"We are not having a massage parlor in Middlemarch," Agnes snapped.

Saber placed the papers on his pile and raised his hands in surrender. "Not my idea."

Valerie set her cup on the saucer with a clink. "Or a wet T—"

"We've received several good ideas. Maybe we could plan events for the rest of the year. Many of the suggestions won't require much organization," Sid interrupted before the discussion changed to town morals. "I'll make a short list for our next meeting, and we can invite the felines who submitted the suggestions to the meeting."

"I thought we were inviting one at a time," Kenneth said.

"Some are youngsters. They might feel more comfortable if they came together," Sid commented.

Saber leaned back in his chair. "That's a good idea."

Valerie nodded. "Get it over in one meeting. Excellent."

"If you'll trust me to make a short list, Saber and I will contact the felines who suggested them," Sid said.

"Fine. Fine." Valerie picked up her handbag and stood. "If you're adding an obstacle course, I'm not going to visit it again."

Saber bit the inside of his lip and managed a quick nod. "So noted."

"Saber Mitchell. I know you're laughing," Agnes said in a stern voice. "If I ever learn who took those photos I swear..."

"It wasn't me," Saber said. "I don't know who took the photos."

Valerie fixed him with a hard stare, her eyes cool behind her glasses. "He truly doesn't know, Agnes. I can tell." She glanced at her watch. "Oh, look at the time. I have a hair appointment. Are you ready to leave, Agnes?"

The two ladies hustled and soon the purr of their vehicle faded into the distance.

"This wet T-shirt contest," Ben said. "Why don't we add it to a picnic day as a bit of fun?"

Saber gaped at Ben. "Pardon?"

"Make a selection of fake bras with weird shapes. Make it funny and humorous. Ask for male and female volunteers and turn it into a competition. Allocate one as a lucky bra and get everyone at the picnic to line up in front of their favorite volunteer. Have a small mystery prize for everyone who chooses the right line. A voucher for a muffin at the café or a free sausage at the sausage sizzle. Something like that."

"It would have to be kid safe," Sid said.

"Organize an event for the kids at the same time. A scavenger hunt or something that will take them away," Ben suggested.

Kenneth tapped his finger on the tabletop. "If we did this, those who suggested the wet T-shirt contest would realize we truly did look at every idea. We're just interpreting it in our way. It'd be a way of getting them to understand we try to listen. A bit of fun."

"You know," Saber said, suppressing his urge to chuckle. "We should dress up in the T-shirts. The council members. Let everyone see we're approachable, willing to listen and have fun."

There was a moment of silence and the elderly felines shared a quick glance before turning back to Saber.

Kenneth stood. "I'd better shift my herd of cows. Brilliant idea. We should do it."

"I vote yes. I'm up for that. Can I catch a ride?" Ben asked Kenneth.

"That is plain crafty, lad. We're in agreement. We'll do it." Sid rose and almost ran to the door to join his two friends. "Since it was your idea, you can tell Valerie and Agnes."

An instant later, the three men vanished, the thud of the front door telling of their rapid departure.

Saber's tongue-in-cheek humor died as he cursed and pushed away his cold cup of tea. "Hell. I walked right into that one." He stood and strode to the fridge to grab a beer. Maybe Emily would help him sell the idea to Valerie and Agnes. After she'd died laughing, of course.

Thank you so much for reading *My Determined Suitor,* and I hope you enjoyed your visit to rural Middlemarch. If you love the book—and the Middlemarch Shifters series—help me spread the word by posting a review or telling your friends.

The real Middlemarch and the south of the South Island are one of my favorite areas of New Zealand to visit, and I have a blast spending time with the Mitchells and their friends. I never know what mischief or drama will occur next. *grin*

Well, not quite true because the next book in the series is *My Cat Burglar*, and it features a cop who is new to the area and a certain male kitty who might (or might not) be doing a little breaking and entering.

Happy reading,

Shelley

About Author

USA Today bestselling author Shelley Munro lives in Auckland, the City of Sails, with her husband and a cheeky Jack Russell/mystery breed dog.

Typical New Zealanders, Shelley and her husband left home for their big OE soon after they married (translation of New Zealand speak - big overseas experience). A twelve-month-long adventure lengthened to six years of roaming the world. Enduring memories include being almost sat on by a mountain gorilla in Rwanda, lazing on white sandy beaches in India, whale watching in Alaska, searching for leprechauns in Ireland, and dealing with ghosts in an English pub.

While travel is still a big attraction, these days Shelley is most likely found in front of her computer following another love - that of writing stories of contemporary and paranormal romance and adventure. Other interests include watching rugby (strictly for research purposes), cycling, playing croquet and the ukelele, and curling up with an enjoyable book.

Visit Shelley at her Website
www.shelleymunro.com

Join Shelley's Newsletter www.shelleymunro.com/newsletter

Visit Shelley's Facebook page
www.facebook.com/ShelleyMunroAuthor

Follow Shelley at Bookbub
www.bookbub.com/authors/shelley-munro

Also By Shelley

Paranormal

Middlemarch Shifters
My Scarlet Woman
My Younger Lover
My Peeping Tom
My Assassin
My Estranged Lover
My Feline Protector
My Determined Suitor
My Cat Burglar
My Stray Cat
My Second Chance
My Plan B
My Cat Nap
My Romantic Tangle
My Blue Lady
My Twin Trouble
My Precious Gift

Middlemarch Gathering
My Highland Mate
My Highland Fling

Middlemarch Capture
Snared by Saber
Favored by Felix
Lost with Leo
Spellbound with Sly
Journey with Joe
Star-Crossed with Scarlett

www.ingramcontent.com/pod-product-compliance
Lightning Source LLC
Chambersburg PA
CBHW022148240626
47153CB00007B/2564